It had been seventeen... come face-to-face wi...

The last time was the day ... graduation—what he'd said to her weeks before was imprinted in her memory like a permanent tattoo.

However, she had to admit time had been extra kind to him, because Fletcher was more handsome than she'd remembered. His large brown eyes with glints of amber appeared to twinkle in amusement in his lean face with its perfectly symmetrical features. His smooth complexion was reminiscent of golden-brown autumn leaves. Their senior class had voted him Best Looking and All-Around Athlete.

"How have you been, Fletcher?"

Nicole did not recognize her own voice because it had dropped an octave. It was obvious after so many years that she was still very attracted to him. He crossed muscular arms over his chest and angled his head. "That's what I should be asking you, Nikki. How are you doing?"

A slight smile parted her lips. "I'm taking it one day at a time."

* * *

WICKHAM FALLS WEDDINGS:
Small-town heroes, bighearted love!

Dear Reader,

You met Nicole Campos briefly in *Claiming the Captain's Baby* and again in *Twins for the Soldier*. And for those who are wondering who the attorney with the USMC tattoo on her wrist is, I've decided to give you a glimpse as to why she returns to Wickham Falls in *This Time for Keeps*.

Nicole's well-ordered life in Florida is turned upside down when she voluntarily gives up her position with a prestigious Miami law firm to return to her hometown. She becomes the temporary guardian for her nephews after her brother is seriously injured in a horrific automobile accident that has claimed the life of his wife and sons' mother. The Falls is a small town where everyone knows one another, but it isn't until Nicole encounters the man who had once—unsuccessfully—asked her to prom that her past comes back to haunt her.

Wounded warrior Special Forces Sergeant Fletcher Austen returned to Wickham Falls to help his father with the family auto repair business and has heard that Nicole is also back. He realizes he has been given a second chance when he offers to stand in as a role model for her nephews during their father's rehabilitation. Although Nicole accepts his offer, Fletcher wonders if his love for her will be enough to convince her to stay, or will he lose her a second time?

Come on back to Wickham Falls, where you will reunite with old friends while at the same time meet new ones who will make you want to know more about them.

Happy reading,

Rochelle Alers

This Time for Keeps

Rochelle Alers

ISBN-13: 978-1-335-57410-7

This Time for Keeps

This edition published by arrangement with Harlequin Books S.A.

For questions and comments about the quality of this book, please contact us at CustomerService@Harlequin.com.

Printed in U.S.A.

Since 1988, national bestselling author **Rochelle Alers** has written more than eighty books and short stories. She has earned numerous honors, including the Zora Neale Hurston Award, the Vivian Stephens Award for Excellence in Romance Writing and a Career Achievement Award from *RT Book Reviews*. She is a member of Zeta Phi Beta Sorority, Inc., Iota Theta Zeta Chapter. A full-time writer, she lives in a charming hamlet on Long Island. Rochelle can be contacted through her website, www.rochellealers.org.

Books by Rochelle Alers

Harlequin Special Edition

Wickham Falls Weddings

Home to Wickham Falls
Her Wickham Falls SEAL
The Sheriff of Wickham Falls

American Heroes

Claiming the Captain's Baby
Twins for the Soldier

Harlequin Kimani Romance

The Eatons

Sweet Silver Bells
Sweet Southern Nights
Sweet Destiny
Sweet Persuasions
Twice the Temptation

Visit the Author Profile page at Harlequin.com for more titles.

Chapter One

Nicole Campos paced the length of the front porch as she waited for the arrival of the local mechanic to check out why her SUV would not start. Any other time she would not have been so anxious, but this morning was different. She was scheduled to appear at the Johnson County courthouse for a hearing that concerned her nephews.

It had been only two months since she'd assumed the role as temporary legal guardian for six-year-old Luke and eight-year-old Daniel Campos after their father had agreed to check into a residential substance abuse treatment facility for his opioid addiction. It had taken several weeks for her brother to agree to sign the documents giving her power of attorney for his finances and custody of his sons until after he'd completed the six-month program.

The sound of an approaching automobile garnered

her attention and she came down off the porch to see a black pickup with Austen Auto & Sons painted on the side door pull up alongside her three-year-old Toyota Pathfinder. Jesse Austen had owned and operated the only auto repair shop in Wickham Falls for decades. There was a running joke throughout the town that every refrigerator door in The Falls had a magnet advertising the business.

Nicole came off the last step at the same time the driver got out of the pickup. Her breath caught in her chest, making it difficult for her to breathe until she was forced to release it. When she'd called and asked for someone to look at her car, the man who'd answered the phone had not told her that one of the owners would come to check it out.

It had been seventeen years since she had come face-to-face with Fletcher Austen. The last time was the day of their high school graduation; what he'd said to her weeks before was imprinted in her memory like a permanent tattoo.

However, she had to admit time had been extra kind to him because Fletcher was more handsome than she'd remembered. His large brown eyes with glints of amber appeared to twinkle in amusement in his lean face with its perfectly symmetrical features. His smooth complexion was reminiscent of golden-brown autumn leaves. Their senior class had voted him Best-Looking and All-Around Athlete.

"How have you been, Fletcher?"

Nicole did not recognize her own voice because it had dropped an octave. It was obvious after so many years that she was still very attracted to him.

He crossed muscular arms over his chest and angled

his head. "That's what I should be asking you, Nikki. How are you doing?"

A slight smile parted her lips. "I'm taking it one day at a time taking care of my nephews."

Day by day meant she no longer had to think of herself. Now she got up earlier than usual to prepare breakfast and make certain her nephews were showered and dressed before the school bus arrived. Now she spent early evenings and afternoons checking homework and/or driving them to their counseling sessions. She had also accepted a temporary part-time position to assist local attorney Preston McAvoy in clearing up a pileup of cases that had resulted when his partner left for another position.

Her annoyance with the vehicle that wouldn't start was exacerbated by her summons to appear in court for a matter that could have been resolved with an in-person meeting. Her brother's in-laws wanted visitation privileges and Nicole would have been more than willing to grant their request without going to court. She knew her nephews' maternal grandparents asking for temporary custodial guardianship was totally monetary based. As a college assistant defensive football coach, her brother, Reggie, earned a mid-six-figure salary. He had complained to her that he'd felt like a personal piggy bank for his wife's family, which was why Nicole had convinced him to agree to permit her to manage his finances until his return.

The day she'd received the telephone call that her brother and his wife had been involved in a vehicular accident—after their minivan had skidded out of control during an ice storm—had changed Nicole's life forever. Her sister-in-law, five months pregnant with her third child, had died at the scene. Reggie had been airlifted to the trauma hospital in the state's capital with broken legs, head injuries and fractured vertebrae.

Reggie, released from hospital after several weeks, had been transferred to a rehabilitation center. His chronic pain had led to an addiction to pain meds and, eventually, to heroin. Months later Nicole, realizing his dependence on drugs was out of control, had arranged, with the assistance of her parents, for him to enter a treatment facility. She'd stayed long enough to resign her position with the Miami law firm she'd worked for, close up her town home and return to West Virginia.

"I'm really sorry to hear about your brother losing Melissa, and his boys their mother."

Nicole nodded. She had lost count of the number of times people had offered their condolences and empathy for the horrific event that had changed her family's dynamics. "Thank you, Fletcher."

He lowered his arms. "What's wrong with your vehicle?"

Nicole lifted her shoulders under the suit jacket. "It just won't start," she said, grateful he had changed the topic.

Fletcher opened the driver's-side door and slipped in behind the wheel. He adjusted the seat to accommodate his longer legs. "The radio works, so I know it's not the battery," he said.

She took a backward step when he got out and opened the hood, forcing herself not to stare at the slim-cut jeans hugging his hips as he leaned over. He'd rolled back the cuffs on his work shirt to reveal strong wrists and forearms with several tattoos. When he'd crossed his arms over his chest, the muscles in his biceps strained against the fabric of the chambray shirt. The last time she'd seen Jesse Fletcher Austen, he was tall, gangly and an incredibly fast sprinter.

As the wide receiver for the school football team, he had broken and set records for two consecutive years. But now, at thirty-five, it was as if he had acquired a monopoly on virility. He had grown a couple of inches; his upper body had filled out and was powerfully muscled. Nicole knew he had been offered athletic scholarships from several colleges but had rejected them all to enlist in the army, which had shocked most folks in The Falls. He had been that good. Two months following their graduation, Fletcher began basic training at Fort Benning, Georgia, as she began her freshman year in the NROTC program at the University of Virginia.

Nicole glanced at her watch. If Fletcher couldn't start the Pathfinder, she would be forced to call the car service in Mineral Springs. She never understood why Wickham Falls did not have a taxi service.

Fletcher stood straight and closed the hood. "All the cables and hoses look okay, so I can't tell what's wrong until it's towed to the shop. We'll have to put it through an electronic diagnostic test."

Nicole ran a hand over her short hair at the same time she smothered a curse under her breath. She shook her head and exhaled. "I don't want to believe this." She looked at her watch again, realizing she had less than thirty minutes to make it to the courthouse. "Tow it, Fletcher."

"Where are you going?" he asked when she turned to go back into the house.

"I have to call Mineral Springs for a taxi. I need to get to the family court by nine thirty."

"Forget the taxi. I'll take you."

Nicole stopped and turned to face Fletcher. "You don't have to do that."

He smiled, bringing her gaze to linger on the elusive dimple in his right cheek. "Yes, I do. After all, it's the least I can do to offer an apology for what I said to you when we were back in school."

She wanted to tell Fletcher there was little he could do to erase the acerbic words. Words that, at seventeen, had made her question her appearance and femininity when she compared herself to some of the more glamorous girls who wore the latest designer fashions and had standing appointments for their hair and nails. It had taken years before Nicole realized her self-worth wasn't about how she looked or what she wore, but her achievements.

"You really don't have to do that, Fletcher," she repeated.

He removed a handkerchief from a pocket of his jeans and wiped his hands. "Yes, I do, Nicole. If we continue to stand here debating how you can get to the courthouse, you'll definitely be late."

She knew he was right and serious when he'd called her Nicole rather than Nikki. Even if she did call for a taxi, she didn't know how long it would take for the dispatcher to send a car to pick her up. "Okay. I need to get my tote from behind the front seat."

Fletcher nodded. "I'll call the shop and have one of the guys tow it."

Nicole retrieved her tote as Fletcher opened the passenger-side door to the pickup. She'd just hiked up the pencil skirt to allow her easier access into the truck when Fletcher's hands circled her waist and lifted her effortlessly until she was settled on the seat.

Her eyes met his. "Thank you." She'd felt the power in his hands as he'd lifted her as easily as he would a child.

Nicole placed the tote on the floor between her feet and then fastened the seat belt. She turned to see Fletcher talking on his cell phone before he got in beside her in the pickup.

Fletcher started up the pickup, put it in Reverse and backed out of the driveway. "I left the doors unlocked and told Billy he'd find the key under the driver's mat." He chanced a quick glance at Nicole as he headed for the county seat.

When the call had come in from Nicole, he'd told his father he would go check on her car. Normally that task would be assigned to one of the two other mechanics, but he knew it would provide him the perfect opportunity to approach Nicole and attempt to make amends for something he'd said more than seventeen years ago.

He'd thought her very cute with her delicate features and her tawny-brown complexion. There were times when she would stare at him with large round brown eyes that seemed much too wise for someone so young. She had always worn her chemically straightened long hair in a ponytail or single braid and the only allowance she made for makeup was lip gloss. However, the woman sitting only inches away had matured appreciably. Subtly applied makeup served to enhance her best features: her eyes and lush lips. The short pixie haircut was the perfect style for her small face.

Fletcher forced himself to keep his eyes on the road

rather than take furtive glances at Nicole's legs in the body-hugging black skirt she had paired with a white man-tailored blouse under the matching jacket. He'd caught glimpses of her in town with her nephews since her return to The Falls, but had decided not to approach her because the timing had not been right.

News had traveled quickly throughout Wickham Falls when Reggie Campos had been seriously injured in an accident that had claimed the life of his young wife a week before Christmas. Residents from The Falls and Mineral Springs had come together to support Melissa Clarke-Campos's family for their loss during what should have been one of the most joyous seasons of the year.

"How long do you plan to stay in The Falls?" Fletcher asked Nicole after a comfortable silence when he stopped at a four-way intersection.

Nicole turned to meet his eyes. "I'll be here until late January or early February. Hopefully by that time Reggie will have successfully completed his rehab."

Fletcher nodded. It was late August, and that meant she would remain in West Virginia for at least the next six months. "Then you're going back to Florida."

"Yes," Nicole said. "Miami is now my home."

He stepped on the gas and executed a smooth left turn onto the two-lane road. "So, do you like living in Miami?"

"Yes," she replied, smiling. "I've gotten used to the summer heat and humidity, and I love the food and the energy of the city."

Fletcher reached for a pair of sunglasses on the console and put them on to shield his eyes against the rays of the sun. "I suppose that's reason enough for not coming back here to live. What about your job?"

"I'll have to look for a new position once I get back. I've exhausted my family-leave privileges and, as a new hire, the senior partners at the firm decided not to authorize a subsequent leave of absence. I don't know if you know, but I'm working for Preston McAvoy while I'm here. It gives me something to do during the day while my nephews are in school."

"I was really surprised when I read in our quarterly graduating class newsletter that you'd left the corps to go to law school."

"I'd promised myself that if I survived my last deployment, I would leave the military. Why did you come back?" Nicole asked.

"I'd planned to become a lifer and then come back to help my brother run the shop once Pop retired. But I was wounded during my third tour and I had to put in for a medical discharge. Even before that my brother decided he preferred working on an oil rig to repairing cars, which meant my plan to serve thirty years was changed to twenty."

Fletcher stared straight ahead. "The doctors were able to save my leg. The scars make it look like a road map, and I find myself limping whenever I'm exhausted, but I'm luckier than many of my buddies who came home missing one or both legs." He heard Nicole's slight intake of breath.

As a Special Forces medical sergeant, he had been responsible for providing initial medical screening to those injured in his unit. The roles were reversed when shrapnel from a rocket-propelled grenade had torn through his right leg, shattering bone and damaging muscle. He'd managed to carry two of his buddies to safety before going into shock. When he woke more than twelve hours later in Landstuhl Regional Medical Center in Kaiserslautern, Germany, he'd been told the prognosis was the possibility of losing the limb. He'd returned to the States and was taken to San Antonio Military Medical Center. After four surgical procedures, he'd finally limped out of the hospital on a cane with the realization his military career had ended.

Fletcher did not want to talk about or to relive his time in the army. He wanted to make amends for what he'd said to Nicole. When it had happened, he hadn't had the courage to apologize to her. "I'm sorry about what I said to you after you told me you wouldn't be my prom date. It was uncalled-for and I never should've said it."

A beat passed. "It's the past, Fletcher, and I'm over it."

He took his eyes off the road for a few seconds. Nicole was so still she could have been carved out of stone and the sentiment in her voice was just as unemotional. "It may be over for you, but not for me, Nikki. When I spent months in the hospital, I had nothing but time to think about my life. What I'd done and things I'd said."

"You said what you meant at the time," Nicole said in a quiet voice, "and my father always told me that whatever comes out of the mouth comes from the heart."

A hint of a smile tilted the corners of Fletcher's mouth. Judge Andrew Campos had earned the reputation of dispensing platitudes to those who appeared in his courtroom before imposing sentence or a fine. "He's right about that. I can't retract what I said, but I know it was immaturity and jealousy that made me lash out at you."

"And don't forget ego," Nicole interjected.

Fletcher had been aware that in high school whenever girls stared at him or remarked about his so-called good looks, he'd found it both uncomfortable and flattering. Once he'd entered adolescence, his father had given him the *talk* about sex. However, it had been his mother who'd warned him about not taking advantage of girls once they began coming to the house or the auto repair shop whenever he spent school recesses and vacations working with his father.

He and Nicole had shared several classes and been on the yearbook and senior class committees, where they had worked closely together on various projects. He hadn't made up his mind about who he'd wanted to take to the prom until three weeks before the event, when he asked Nicole if she would be his date. She had declined his invitation and a part of him hadn't been able to accept that she had rejected him. In the end, she had gone with a boy who'd lived next door to her.

At the time, he had been all ego, because not only was he an above-average student, popular with both boys and girls, and he was also a standout on the gridiron—all of which served to inflate his sense of self. It had taken age and maturity to for him to realize what he'd said to Nicole was not only cruel, but totally uncalled-for.

He nodded, realizing he had to accept the truth. "You're right. It was more ego than anything else."

Nicole did not want to dredge up the past, but knew if she was going to spend six months in Wickham Falls and would probably run into Fletcher, they had to settle their past. "You were so used to girls falling over themselves to get you to notice them that you couldn't accept that I'd rejected your invitation to go to prom with you."

"It wasn't only that, Nikki."

Shifting slightly on the seat, Nicole turned to look directly at him. "What else was there?"

"It's what you said when you accused me of sleeping with a number of cheerleaders at the same time. And, for your information, I'd never slept with any girl who went to our school."

She went completely still. "If that's the case then why did you say, 'What's the matter, Nikki? Are you jealous I didn't ask you to sleep with me?'"

Fletcher shook his head. "I don't know."

Her eyebrows lifted slightly. "You don't know. Had you found me so unattractive that you couldn't see yourself sleeping with me?"

"No, no," he said quickly. "It was just the opposite. I'd always thought you were one of the smartest and prettiest girls in the school, but I was afraid to ask you out because of your father."

Nicole stared at Fletcher as if he had taken leave of his senses. Andrew Campos had been the local judge for the first ten years of her life before being appointed to the criminal court in the state capital. "What did my father have to do with anything?"

There was a swollen silence until Fletcher said, "Did you ever wonder why most of the boys at the school wouldn't talk to you?"

"No. Why wouldn't they?"

Fletcher smiled. "They were afraid of Judge Campos."

Her jaw dropped. "Are you saying they viewed my father as some kind of monster?"

"Not a monster, Nikki. Just someone they didn't want

to have to deal with in case you told him a boy had attempted to take advantage of you."

"That's absurd. And you weren't afraid of having to face him when you asked me to prom?"

His smile grew wider. "No, because I knew it would be the first and hopefully not the last time I'd ask you out on a date. And besides, I wouldn't have done anything you hadn't wanted me to do."

"Like sleep with me?"

"I told you before, I didn't sleep with any girl from our school, and I had no intention of starting with you."

Nicole felt a modicum of relief he hadn't thought of her as a "judge's daughter" trophy about which he could brag to his buddies. And Fletcher had been truthful about boys either not talking to or coming on to her. There were occasions she'd felt totally isolated when her female classmates gave her smug stares because she wouldn't have to compete with them for the attention of the more popular boys. Her best friend had been the boy who'd lived across the street from her and who'd confided to her that even though he was attracted to the same sex he was afraid to come out; she was the perfect foil for his proclivity.

"Thank you for being truthful," she said as she forced a smile.

"Does this mean you're going to accept my apology?"

"As I said before, it's the past, Fletcher."

"It's either yes or no, Nikki."

Nicole turned and stared out the side window at the passing landscape. If Fletcher wanted absolution for his remark, then she would offer it. "Yes, Fletcher, I forgive you."

She quickly dismissed his apology, pondering the issue of having to deal with her brother's in-laws. She now understood Reggie's dilemma whenever he called to talk about his wife's family. There was never a time he did not complain about the drain on his finances when writing checks to cover the Clarkes' bills. Nicole had not wanted to get involved in what could possibly become a family feud, so she'd offered him little or no advice on how to deal with the Clarkes.

"Are your parents enjoying their retirement?"

Fletcher's question broke into Nicole's musings.

Once her parents had retired, they gave Reggie and Melissa their house as a wedding gift. She smiled. "Oh, yes. They're like kids in a candy shop. They live in a gated retirement community with every amenity you'd want and need. Dad offers legal advice pro bono for at-risk youth, while my mother volunteers tutoring those studying for the LSAT. They claim it's their way of giving back." Her smile faded. "But whenever I talk to Mom, I can hear sadness in her voice when she talks about Reggie. She claims she prays every day that he will make it through his first ninety days without relapsing." Her brother had managed to hide his addiction from those in The Falls until he'd overdosed and been transported to the hospital.

"Is she able to see him?" Fletcher questioned.

"No."

"Isn't that rather restrictive for family members?"

"Yes and no. Yes, because it keeps families in limbo as to the patient's progress. No, because some may be complicit in aiding their addiction. Once I told my parents that Reggie needed in-patient rehab treatment, they found a private facility less than a mile from where they live. Convincing him to go was like attempting to pull an impacted wisdom tooth with a pair of tweezers."

Fletcher asked her yet another question. "What did you do to convince him?"

"He knew he needed help after his sons found him unresponsive on the bathroom floor with a hypodermic in his arm. They were so traumatized that I decided to put them into counseling."

"Good for you, Nikki. Addiction is a disease that affects the entire family."

"You're so right about that," she said softly, knowing Reggie's addiction to opiates had affected not only his children, parents and sister, but also his in-laws.

"You can let me out here and I'll walk to the courthouse," Nicole told Fletcher when he turned into the designated public parking lot. "I appreciate you dropping me off. I'll take a taxi back to The Falls."

"You don't have to do that. I'll drive you back," Fletcher volunteered. "I'll wait here while you defend your client."

Nicole met his eyes. "I'm the client."

"You're joking, aren't you?"

"I wish," she countered. "My nephews' grandparents are suing me because they want court-ordered visitation."

"Have you kept them from seeing the boys?"

"No, but it's a lot more complicated than that."

"If that's the case, then I'm coming in with you."

She smiled and rested her hand on his forearm. "I can assure you that I don't need backup."

Fletcher stared at her hand. "If you have to deal with folks from Mineral Springs, then you're going to need someone to have your back."

"Don't be silly, Fletcher. This is not some football game between rival teams." No one could pinpoint when the football rivalry between Wickham Falls and Mineral Springs had begun, but it had been evident when she was in high school, and rumor was that it persisted more than a decade and a half later.

"It doesn't matter," Fletcher said as he pulled into an empty parking space and shut off the engine. "I'm still going in with you."

Nicole did not want to argue with him when she had to keep her head straight to defend her decision against the lawyer the Clarkes had hired to represent them. "Okay. Come with me."

For the second time that morning, she had conceded to Fletcher, something she had only done in the past with her commanding officers. As a former captain in the corps, she was used to giving orders and having them followed without question. But she was no longer active military, just a civilian attorney who had resigned her position as an associate with a prestigious Miami-based law firm to take care of her family.

Chapter Two

Nicole stood in the designated line for attorneys and court personnel. She showed one of the court officers her credentials, allowed him to examine the contents of her tote and was waved through. She watched as Fletcher removed his belt and placed his keys and cell phone in a small plastic container before he was allowed to pass through the checkpoint and join her.

"I wonder how many people actually bring weapons into a courthouse," he said as he slipped on his belt.

"You'd be surprised," she said. She walked over to the board where various dockets were posted. "Even though we have a concealed carry law in the state, folks take that to mean they can bring their firearms everywhere." Nicole perused the board and found her name. "I'm in courtroom two."

Fletcher fell into step with her. "When I read in our

high school graduating class newsletter that you were a lawyer, I was surprised you hadn't become JAG."

Nicole wanted to tell Fletcher that she had had enough of the military. Although she had served honorably and with distinction, after several deployments and attending military funerals or witnessing comrades battling PSTD, she'd realized she wanted out. "As I said before, it's the past, Fletcher." Once she'd filed the separation papers to become a civilian, Nicole had never looked back.

"I'm sorry for prying."

She smiled up at Fletcher. "There's no need to apologize. I'm just not ready to talk about it now. But once I straighten out this dilemma and clear my head, I'll tell you everything."

Fletcher rested a hand at the small of her back. "No rush."

"Thank you."

Nicole walked into the courtroom, Fletcher following, and avoided the hostile stares of the Clarkes as she took her seat opposite them. The elder Clarkes, Johnnie Lee and Bessie, along with their adult son, Jamal, and daughter-in-law, Brandy, were in attendance.

There were three other cases on the docket before she was called. As the defendant, she hadn't had to prepare an opening statement. She just had to tell the truth when asked. The Clarkes' dapper lawyer put on a performance that was so theatrical it was laughable.

"They lost their only daughter and her unborn baby in a horrific accident and the only things they have of hers to hold on to are their grandsons."

It was obvious the judge was used to his performance. She stopped him halfway through his monologue when he accused Nicole of not sharing her nephews with their aunt, uncle, cousins and grandparents. "That will be all, Mr. Halloran. Is this true, Miss Campos?" the judge questioned Nicole.

"No, it is not, Your Honor. The court is aware that my brother has given me temporary custodial responsibility of his minor sons, and that I also have power of attorney for his business finances until he completes a six-month program for his substance abuse. At no time have I prevented the Clarkes from seeing their grandsons."

"What the boys need is a positive male role model, not some unmarried ex-Marine lady captain who believes she knows what it takes to raise boys," Jamal Clarke shouted.

Nicole gave her nephews' uncle what she thought of as her death stare. "My marital status should not be a factor when it comes to taking care of *my* nephews."

"Your Honor. May I address the court?" Everyone turned to stare at Fletcher when he stood up.

The judge peered over her half-glasses at Fletcher. She nodded. "Can you please state your name for the record?"

"Jesse Fletcher Austen."

The judge nodded again. "What do you want to say, Mr. Austen?"

Fletcher met Nicole's eyes for a brief moment. "I don't mean to usurp Miss Campos's responsibility in caring for her nephews, but I'm volunteering to step in as a male role model until their father returns."

Judge Nelson narrowed her eyes. "Why do you believe you would be a positive role model for the minor Campos boys?"

"I was a US Army Special Forces medical sergeant

for fifteen years. During my last tour, I was wounded in combat, awarded a Purple Heart and Bronze Star and a medical discharge."

"What is your connection to Miss Campos?" Mr. Halloran asked.

The judge held up her hand. "Careful, Mr. Halloran. Right now, I'm the one asking the questions. Mr. Austen, are you in a relationship with Miss Campos?"

Fletcher shook his head. "No, Your Honor. Nicole and I are good friends. We went to high school together."

The judge smiled. "I applaud you and Miss Campos for your service to our country." Her smile faded when she looked at the Clarkes. "Mr. Halloran, I suggest you talk to your clients and get them to agree to something that is amenable to Miss Campos."

"I'm willing to have the boys spend every other weekend with their grandparents, or whenever there is a school holiday or recess," Nicole said quickly. "The exception will be the Christmas recess, when I plan to take them to Florida to visit with their paternal grandparents. I can drop them off on Fridays around 6:00 p.m. and pick them up at the same time on Sunday evenings."

The middle-aged lawyer with a mouth filled with shockingly white porcelain veneers smiled. "Please give me a few minutes to confer with my clients." It took less than a minute for him to come to a consensus with those he represented. "My clients have agreed to Miss Campos's arrangement for visitation."

The judge banged her gavel. "This case is concluded."

Nicole walked over to her nephews' grandfather. Her eyes were drawn to the noticeable scar above the tall dark-skinned man's left eye. Johnnie Lee Clarke, a Vietnam veteran, had earned a reputation as a brawler in his younger days. It had taken him a long time to come to the realization that he had no tolerance for alcohol and finally give it up altogether. He wouldn't allow anything stronger than pop in his home.

"We could have solved this if you had come to me directly rather than spend money to hire a lawyer," she said to the older man.

Johnnie ran a large hand over his shaved pate. "When I asked you to leave the boys with us before you drove Reggie to Florida, you said you couldn't do that."

"Did you forget that I told you I didn't want the last image Luke and Danny had of their father to be of him lying unconscious on the bathroom floor? The doctors had prescribed enough methadone for Reggie until his intake, which gave the boys time to hang out with him without the fear of him 'getting sick' again and having to give himself a needle filled with medicine to make him well." She'd hated lying to the boys, but at their age she hadn't wanted to expose them to the awareness that their father was addicted to heroin.

"I just thought you didn't want them to have anything to do with us."

"Well, you're wrong, Johnnie. We're family, and the sooner you realize that, everything will go well with us." She knew if the Clarkes were given custody of their grandsons, then they would receive money from the state as their foster parents.

Johnnie extended a large gnarled hand. "I'm sorry, Nicole."

She ignored the proffered hand, went on tiptoe and kissed his cheek. "Apology accepted. I'll bring the boys over Friday."

"What about the Labor Day weekend? You know we

always have an end-of-the-summer cookout that weekend. And the kids don't have classes on Tuesday because teachers have professional development."

"Okay. You can have them this weekend and the next one." Turning on her heel, she walked over to Fletcher. "I'm ready to leave now."

He took her free hand. Nicole felt the calluses on Fletcher's hand as he gave her fingers a gentle squeeze. It was obvious he was no stranger to working with his hands. She'd noticed that, despite being a mechanic, he didn't have dirt under his fingernails.

"It looks as if you made peace with Grandpa Clarke," Fletcher remarked.

"Let's see how long it will last. His wife and son didn't look very happy, but there's nothing they can do about it because now they'll have to abide by today's determination." Nicole waited until they were seated in the pickup to ask Fletcher, "What made you volunteer to become a temporary foster father for my nephews?"

Throwing back his head, Fletcher laughed loudly. "Is that what I am?"

"What else are you, Fletcher, if you're willing to stand in as a temporary dad?"

"I suppose you're right about that. Maybe I can get some practice in before I decide to become a father."

"You don't have any children?" Her voice rose slightly with the query.

"Nope."

"Why not? What are you waiting for?"

A beat passed. "Before I answer your question, I'd like you to answer one for me."

"What is it?" she asked.

"Why don't you have any children?"

Nicole stared straight ahead for several seconds before saying, "I haven't met the man I'd want to father my children."

She couldn't admit to Fletcher that she had met someone she would have considered marrying if their circumstances had been different. He was an enlisted man, though not in her unit. Fraternizing with him would have jeopardized her commission, so she'd been forced to conceal her feelings for him. Back then she hadn't been ready to sacrifice her military career for love.

"You've never been in love?" Fletcher asked.

She turned to study his distinctive profile. "Not really."

Fletcher's eyebrows lifted slightly. "Either it's yes or no."

"Yes, but it wasn't able to be reciprocated."

"By you or him?"

"For both of us."

Fletcher drove another quarter of a mile before he said, "You were an officer and he wasn't."

She smiled. "You're quite perceptive."

"I'm not that perceptive. I've just seen my share of commissioned and noncommissioned officers having to hide their liaisons. If he had been an officer, would you have married him?" Fletcher questioned.

"I would if he had been in love with me."

"Are you saying your relationship was that one-sided? That you loved him but he didn't love you?"

"Just say that he liked me and I liked him, and leave it at that. What about you, Fletcher? Why haven't you married?"

"I had a few relationships over the years, but none of them reached the point where I would've considered proposing marriage. And it wasn't even an option as long as I was deployed. Wickham Falls has had its share of military widows and I wouldn't want my wife to have to raise our children by herself."

Nicole had attended school with students who'd lost a father, brother or uncle while serving in the military, and the impact had been devastating for their families. The names of the deceased veterans were added to the granite memorial erected at the end of Main Street and honored every year during Memorial Day celebrations.

"I think you should come and meet my nephews," Nicole said, deftly changing the topic of conversation. She did not feel comfortable allowing Fletcher to interact with Daniel and Luke without her being present.

Fletcher nodded. "That sounds like a good idea. When do you want to introduce me to them?"

"Maybe you can come over for dinner before Friday."

"What about tomorrow?"

"Tomorrow works for me," Nicole said in agreement. "We usually sit down for dinner around six. Is that too early for you?"

Fletcher wanted to tell Nicole it was, but knew he had to compromise. Most nights he worked until six and then went home to shower and prepare dinner. He'd made it a habit to eat while viewing the nightly news, following with several sport channels to unwind from the day's events. Weekends were his to do whatever he wanted. The shop was not open on Saturdays or Sundays and that was his time to work on his current restoration project.

"No," he said. "Six is okay."

"I said six because I try to keep the boys on a schedule that works for them. Luke has to be in bed by eight because he needs at least ten hours of sleep or he's out of sorts in the morning, while Daniel has a ten o'clock curfew."

"What time do you get them up for school?"

"I don't. Both have alarm clocks and I expect them to get up on their own. Without the clocks they would probably stay in bed until noon."

Fletcher signaled and turned off onto the road leading to the town limits for Wickham Falls. "Are you saying it took a marine captain to whip them into shape?"

Her throaty laugh filled the interior of the truck. "I try not to ride them too hard. I don't want my nephews to think of me as a bully, because they've gone through so much at such an early age. They've lost their mother and their father will be away for the next six months, so I'm very careful when I explain why I want or need them to do something for me."

"Do they give you a hard time?"

"Surprisingly no. My sister-in-law wasn't what you would call a gourmet cook and, compared to her, I'm a celebrity chef."

"Are you saying you're a fabulous cook?"

"Not quite fabulous, but good enough. I include their suggestions as to what they want for dinner and weekend brunch, which makes them agreeable to other things I ask of them."

Fletcher flashed a wide grin. "If that's the case, then I'm looking forward to tomorrow." The ringtone on his cell phone revealed he had a text message. Signaling again, he pulled off the road and took out his phone. "Billy just sent me a text saying a component in the ignition has to be replaced. Do you want him to order the part?"

"Of course," Nicole said. "I need my car."

Fletcher tapped the keys, giving Billy the approval, and then waited for a reply. "It's expected to be delivered on Thursday."

Nicole groaned softly. "I'm certain Preston McAvoy can do without me for a couple of days, but I need to take the boys to counseling on Thursday," she said under her breath. "I have to rent a car because I don't want them to miss their sessions."

"Forget about renting a car, Nikki. I have a loaner you can use until yours is repaired."

"I really don't want to put you out any more than I have."

"Have you been gone so long that you've forgotten that folks in The Falls always look out for one another?"

"No, but—"

"No *buts*, Nikki," Fletcher said, interrupting her. "You may have outranked me in the military, but as civilians we should be able to have sensible discussions as equals."

"Old habits die hard, Fletcher."

He nodded. "Tell me about it. There are times when I still act like a sergeant barking orders and Pop has to remind me that I'm no longer in the army."

"I've been out of the corps longer than you have the army and I still find myself thinking like a marine."

"Were you strictly a by-the-book soldier?"

"I never thought of myself as one, but then you would have to ask some that I served with. Even though women have risen to become generals, there is still a stigma about women serving in the military. When I first became a helicopter pilot, I was assigned to extracting the wounded in the field before I graduated to piloting Blackhawk helicopter gunships during airstrikes."

"If you'd stayed in, you probably could've risen to the rank of at least a lieutenant colonel."

"I was really striving for general."

A knowing smile spread over Fletcher's features. The girl he'd known in high school hadn't changed that much. When they'd talked about the military Nicole had always said she'd wanted to become a general, because there were too few women who'd attained the rank. And he had no doubt that if she had remained in the corps, she would have reached her goal.

"Wickham Falls has never had a general. Aiden Gibson was a navy SEAL. Sawyer Middleton was an army electronic intelligence technician. Sheriff Seth Collier a marine MP and Leland Remington an army ranger. And there's also Dr. Dwight Adams, who is a major in the army reserves. Now you're back as a captain."

"Only temporarily, Fletcher. The Falls has another marine captain in Giles Wainwright."

Fletcher started the pickup, waited for a lull in oncoming traffic and maneuvered back onto the road. "Have you met him?"

"Yes. I met him after I'd begun working for Preston."

"Do you like working for him?" Preston had taken over the family-based law firm once he'd graduated law school and passed the West Virginia bar. Preston's great-grandfather had defended striking miners charged with assaulting strikebreakers and the goons protecting them.

"I do. He asked me to help him out with a backlog of cases once he'd heard that I was going to be here through the new year. I told him I could only give him five hours a day because I need to be home to see my nephews off to school and be at home when the bus drops them off. He said he would accept whatever help I could give him."

"How does it compare to the work you did in Florida?" Fletcher asked.

"There is no comparison, Fletcher. As an associate for a large firm, I'd work on average fifty and sometimes sixty hours a week. I'd arrive home so exhausted that all I'd do was shower and fall into bed."

"What about your social life?"

"I didn't have much of one."

"No boyfriend?"

She shook her head. "No. I didn't have time to devote to a normal relationship."

Fletcher gave Nicole a sidelong glance. "Maybe that will change now that you're here."

"I don't think so, Fletcher. I'm not going to get involved with someone and then break it off when I leave next year."

"Maybe something will happen that will force you to change your mind and you'll decide to stay."

"Bite your tongue, Jesse Fletcher Austen. What are you trying to do? Jinx me?"

He chuckled, the sound seemingly coming from his chest. "Why did you have to go and use my entire government name?"

"Well, it did get your attention. If you were named after your father, why didn't they call you Junior instead of Fletcher?"

"You'll have to ask my parents about that," Fletcher said. "My father said if he had a son, he wanted him to carry on the name given to him, while my mother hated calling me Junior. She started calling me Fletcher and it stuck."

"If I have a son, I'd never consider naming him after his father because I believe a child should have his own identity. Speaking of sons, I have to tell you that I have a fur baby."

"You have a dog?" Fletcher asked.

Nicole nodded. "Yes. I brought him back with me the last time I went to Florida."

"Are you allowed to have dogs where you live?"

"Yes."

"Is he a rescue?"

"Not really. He belonged to a friend who was unable to care for him, so I offered to take him."

"How old and what breed?"

"Othello is a five-year-old Belgian Malinois."

"He's former military." Fletcher's query was a statement.

"Yes. His handler was a SEAL who has been diagnosed with severe PTSD. During his dark moods he'd forget to walk or feed Othello, and that's when his sister asked me if I would take Othello."

"How do your nephews get along with the dog?"

"They love him. It took a while before Othello warmed up to them, but now they're besties."

"I'm also looking forward to meeting Othello." Fletcher wondered if the SEAL had been Nicole's romantic interest, which had led her to accept the responsibility of adopting his specially trained military dog.

Suddenly it hit him. Nicole had unselfishly given up a promising position with a Miami-based law firm to oversee the well-being of her nephews. She had also agreed to adopt a canine that would be hard to place with a family because he had been trained for warfare. Not only were military dogs large and powerful, but also very well-trained and disciplined. She had sacrificed much and hopefully it would not all be in vain.

"Is it possible for me to meet Othello today?"

"You're not in a hurry to get back to the garage?"

Fletcher shook his head. "Not really. When I left, there was only one car in the bay that needed work. And the place definitely will not fall apart if I'm not there."

"What about your father?"

"Pop will hang around until I get back. He spends most of the day in the office recliner watching television. A few times I found him asleep, but he denies it and claims he was just resting his eyes."

"If that's the case, then are you willing to stay long enough to share lunch with me?" Nicole asked. "It's the least I can do to repay you for driving me to the courthouse."

"You really don't have to repay me, Nikki, but I will accept your invitation."

Fletcher did not want to tell Nicole that she was making it easy for him to reconnect with her so they could possibly resume their former friendship. She didn't know he was willing to do anything for her if only to absolve himself of the cutting accusation he'd flung at her in what now seemed half a lifetime ago.

The instant those words had rolled off his tongue, he'd regretted it, especially when he'd detected her shocked expression and the obvious pain in her eyes as they'd filled with unshed tears. Every time he'd seen her in the following weeks, she'd averted her eyes rather that meet his.

They had graduated, leaving Fletcher filled with guilt that had lingered with him for years. He could not turn back the clock or retract what he'd said, but he had promised himself that he would do everything possible or within reason to regain her confidence.

"Don't move. I'll help you down," he said to Nicole as he pulled into the driveway to her home and shut off the engine. He knew the pickup's oversize tires made accessing and exiting the vehicle a little problematic for someone of her height. He also knew the slimness of her skirt would make it even more difficult for her.

Assisting Nicole also gave Fletcher the opportunity to touch her and inhale the sensual perfume on her body, which brought back memories of when they'd worked closely together on high school committees. His fondest memory of Nicole was how wonderful she'd smelled. She would occasionally change fragrances and he'd thought each one was the perfect complement for her body's natural scent.

He successfully hid a smile when his hands circled her waist and he held her against his chest for several seconds, luxuriating in her warmth and the soft curves molded to his upper body. "There you go," he said glibly, setting her on her feet.

Nicole met his eyes. "Thank you."

Fletcher inclined his head. "You're most welcome." He waited for her to retrieve her tote, closed the truck door and followed her up the porch to the house and inside once she disabled the security system. He had only taken a step when he saw the dog.

Chapter Three

"Can I pet him?"

Nicole kicked off her heels and left them on a thick mat, setting the tote on the bench seat in the entryway. "No. Let him come to you to get your scent."

Fletcher stared at the brown, black and gold dog. Belgian Malinois didn't weigh as much as German shepherds, which made them easier to carry over their handler's shoulders or when executing a halo jump. "What happens after he gets my scent?"

Nicole removed her suit jacket and left it on the bench, drawing Fletcher's gaze to linger on the roundness of her breasts under the white blouse. He looked away before she could find him staring at her petite, compact body. Although standing no taller than five-three, she appeared to be in incredible shape and he wondered if she worked out.

Unbuttoning the cuffs to her blouse, Nicole rolled back

the sleeves. "He'll follow you around for a while and, once he gets used to you, and if you're seated, he will rest his muzzle on your thigh. Until then, I suggest you give him the space he needs to decide if he likes you."

Fletcher wiped his booted feet on the mat. "And if he doesn't?"

"Then he won't let you come through the front door."

"The fact that he hasn't attacked me means I have a fifty-fifty chance of being accepted."

Nicole smiled. "He's not going to attack you. Othello is very protective of me and the boys. Even before I brought him home to live with me, I had to spend time with him at my friend's house so he could get used to me. Military dogs usually form unbreakable bonds with their human partners, so separating from Keith wasn't easy for him. He's allowed the run of this house, but the kitchen is off-limits because the boys like to feed Othello from the table."

Fletcher nodded. It was the first time Nicole had referred to the former SEAL by his given name. "Once you forge a bond with someone, whether human or animal, separating can be somewhat difficult."

It was Nicole's turn to nod. "I hope you like meat loaf, because I usually save enough from the night before to have it for next day's lunch."

"I can assure you that I eat any and everything."

"I like a man who's not a picky eater," Nicole said.

"If that's the case, then you'll definitely like me."

Nicole gave him a long, penetrating stare. "What makes you believe that I don't like you?"

The instant she'd asked the question, Nicole wondered what had made her ask him that. The fact was she did like Fletcher. A lot. And it wasn't the teenage crush she'd had in what now seemed like eons ago, but as an adult woman who'd found herself attracted to a man. When she'd reassured Fletcher that what he'd said to her was the past, she'd meant it. At that time, she had been so adversely affected by his insult that it had taken a while before she had gained enough confidence to discover men *were* attracted to her. She'd witnessed death and dying, faced death more times than she could count or remember, so an adolescent boy's inability to accept rejection had rarely entered her consciousness.

Fletcher angled his head as he stood straight and clasped his hands behind his back. His stance reminded her of those standing at ease. It was obvious old habits were slow to die. "I don't know, Nikki. You tell me you're over what I'd said to you, but somehow I don't believe it."

Nicole turned on the heels of her bare feet. "Come with me, Fletcher, and we'll talk while I prepare lunch… Are you coming?" she asked over her shoulder when he didn't move.

"Yes, Captain Campos."

She stopped, turned and gave him a lethal stare. "If you call me that again, I will jack you up," she said teasingly, a hint of a smile playing at the corners of her mouth.

Fletcher slowly shook his head. "I don't think so. I'm at least a foot taller and probably outweigh you by a hundred pounds, and you think you can jack me up. Don't forget I was Special Forces."

"And don't you forget that marines are the best when it comes to hand-to-hand combat," she said with a broad grin. She'd become proficient in throwing techniques as a student of judo.

It was Fletcher's turn to smile. "I'll try to remember that when I toss you up in the air like a beach ball."

Nicole winked at him. "We'll continue this later. I don't know about you, but I need to eat. Whenever I'm stressed out I eat."

"You must not get stressed out too much, because you're definitely not overweight."

"That's because I run every day, rain or shine. I leave the office at two, come home and change and Othello and I go for a run before the school bus drops Luke and Danny off around three thirty."

"You have me there, because I don't run anymore. I can walk at least a mile before I begin limping."

She went completely still. Nicole chided herself for teasing Fletcher about jacking him up. She'd forgotten he had a permanent injury. "What about pain?"

"What about it, Nikki?"

"Do you have pain in your leg?"

"It only bothers me when I overdo it."

"I'm sorry about teasing you about jacking you up. Please come into the kitchen with me, Fletcher. All I had this morning was a cup of black coffee and right now the caffeine is eating a hole in my stomach."

Fletcher moved closer and dropped a kiss on the top of her head. "Okay." Othello moved closer and growled a bit. "What's the matter with him?"

"Othello is a little overprotective. He gets upset when anyone other than Luke or Danny comes too close to me. But don't worry because he won't attack you or anyone unless I give him the command."

He put up his hands in a gesture of surrender. "Sorry, buddy, I won't touch her again."

Fletcher followed Nicole into a fully functional kitchen with state-of-the-art appliances. Even if he'd wanted to touch Nicole, he knew that wasn't possible with Othello growling at him. He had seen firsthand the serious wounds that military dogs inflicted on an enemy.

"This is nice," he said under his breath as Nicole washed her hands in a small prep sink and dried them on a paper towel. "You must do some serious cooking in here."

She opened the French-door fridge and removed several covered dishes. "I try. My parents renovated the kitchen before they decided they wanted to relocate. My grandmother came to live with us once Mom went back to work. By the time I was fourteen, I was able to put an entire meal on the table and that included soup, salad, entrée, homemade bread and dessert."

"Hot damn!" Fletcher mumbled. "You have no idea how many women I've met who claim they only know how to make reservations."

"In defense of my sisters, you need to know that we also have careers that leave little or no time to bake bread."

Resting his elbows on the granite countertop, Fletcher met her eyes over the cooking island. "A relationship isn't about one person but two, Nikki. And that means sharing the responsibility of taking care of their children and picking up the slack when it comes to cooking or cleaning the house."

Nicole opened the dish with the meat loaf and the ingredients she had seasoned the meat with wafted to his nostrils. She removed the top of another dish filled with sweet potato wedges and then a third with red cabbage.

"You appear to be the exception rather than the norm, Fletcher. I spent more than a dozen years with some men who reminded me every day of their contempt for a female commanding officer and that they'd rather see me barefoot and pregnant. Women are now CEOs, have run for president, become astronauts, sit on the Supreme Court, and still, we have to be twice as good as our male counterparts."

Rising slightly and reaching over the countertop, Fletcher captured her right wrist and stared at the USMC tattooed on the underside. He then quickly released her when he remembered her warning about Othello's reaction to touching her. "You're preaching to the choir, Nikki. I do cook a little and I'm willing to help you out whenever you need a sous chef. And I'm committed to helping you with your nephews until Reggie completes treatment."

Her hands stilled. "Why, Fletcher?"

"I'm surprised you have to ask," he countered.

"But I am asking."

Fletcher knew what he was about to tell Nicole would no doubt shock her, but she had to know how he felt about her. It had been seventeen years since they were in school together and, unknowingly, he had found himself comparing every woman he'd met since that time to her. He had always liked Nicole but, like so many boys, he'd been reluctant to invite her out on a date because of her father. Prom, however, had given him the perfect excuse, though he'd had no way of knowing that she was going with a boy who lived on her street.

"Even though you were quiet and didn't hang out with some of our classmates after football games, I got to see another side of you when we were on the yearbook and senior class committees. That's when I knew I really liked you."

"Was it because I didn't flirt with you?"

Fletcher nodded. "I must admit you were a challenge."

"Challenge or not, I had no intention of going out with you, even if I hadn't had a prom date, because I'd promised myself to never date a jock."

"I wasn't a jock," he said defensively.

"What else were you, Fletcher? You were the wide receiver for the school's football team. And rumors were going around that the boys on the football and baseball teams were competing with one another as to how many girls they could sleep with before graduation."

Fletcher had known a few guys who'd kept count of the number of virgins they'd had sex with and then bragged openly about it. "You're right about that. But not everyone was doing it."

"It didn't matter," Nicole said, "but I wasn't willing to go into a situation where I'd have to fight off some dude who felt he could force me go to bed with him. And I didn't want a repeat with Reggie after Traci's brother nearly beat Scott Remsen to death after he took advantage of her."

Fletcher remembered the incident that had caused a schism between neighboring families when Traci Miller accused Scott of rape. Scott had been charged with sexual assault and Traci's brother with attempted murder. It was enough to curtail the romantic antics of many of the athletes for the remainder of the school year. Nicole's brother, three years her senior, had been awarded a full athletic scholarship to play football as defensive linebacker at Virginia Tech and had always been very protective of his younger sister.

"Are you saying if I hadn't been a jock you would've gone to prom with me?"

She glanced up, meeting his eyes. "No."

He sat straight on the stool. "Really?"

"Don't look so shocked, Fletcher. You seemed so full of yourself that you thought you could get any girl you wanted. And it did not matter to me that you were voted best-looking. I still wouldn't have dated you."

"Well, damn," Fletcher quipped. "I had no inkling you thought of me like that."

"If you'd asked, I would've told you," Nicole countered. "High school should've been fun, but for me it was just the opposite. And because both my parents were lawyers, some of the kids felt I should've gone to private school. When I got a car for my sixteenth birthday, I truly became an outsider."

"I'm sorry, Nikki. I wasn't aware you had to go through all that. I just thought it was because your father was a criminal court judge that kids kept their distance."

"It didn't matter then, and it still doesn't matter. Mom always told me I was unique. The instant I received my lieutenant's bars, I felt it for the first time."

Fletcher watched Nicole as she preheated the stovetop griddle. She appeared quite comfortable in the kitchen when she placed the cabbage in a microwave dish and the fries on a baking sheet in the oven. "Becoming a commissioned officer is quite a feat."

"Why didn't you apply for Officer's Candidate School?" she asked.

He lifted his shoulders. "I'd thought about it a few

times, but once I decided I wanted to be Special Forces, I knew I'd found my niche. I suppose I was an adrenaline junkie because I was always ready to accept a challenge that entailed danger, and I had to make certain to stay in top physical condition."

Her hands stilled. "What I don't understand is why you turned down full college scholarships to enlist in the military."

Fletcher stared over her shoulder at the clock on the microwave. "I never told anyone—not even my parents—but just before we made it to the state championship, a defensive lineman's helmet hit mine and I went down like a ton of bricks. I was diagnosed with a mild concussion and plagued with headaches for a couple of weeks. I managed to suck it up and went back on the gridiron. Fortunately, it was the last game and we won the championship, but then I'd told myself never again. That's why I declined the scholarships. Another hit to the head and I'd probably end up brain damaged."

"Would you allow your son to play football?"

"No."

"You sound like my brother. Even though he coaches college ball, he says he would never permit his sons to play the game."

"Smart man."

Fletcher recalled the times when he'd come home after a game, aching all over, and would sit the tub with ice to offset the pain. He knew he had disappointed his parents, his father in particular, who'd hoped he would make it to the NFL, but he'd been too cowardly to talk to them about the blinding headaches that plagued him when he least expected. And not once did he ever regret enlisting in the army.

Reaching into an overhead cabinet, Nicole took down plates and glasses. "What would you like to drink?"

"What are the choices?"

"Water, lemonade and pop. I got rid of the beer and alcohol because Reggie was using them to get high."

"I'll have water. Speaking of beer, did you know that the Wolf Den has designated Mondays as Military Monday? Anyone active or former military can eat and drink half-off everything, as long as you wear something identifying your branch."

"How often do you go?" Nicole asked.

"I try to make it a couple of times a month just for the camaraderie."

"I haven't done any socializing since I've been back."

"What about Labor Day?"

"Labor Day may work because I promised Grandpa Clarke he could have the boys that weekend."

Fletcher's smile was dazzling. "Are we on for Military Monday?"

"Yes." She had packed several T-shirts with the corps insignia she usually wore while doing housework and she had a cap that matched the fatigues she'd worn when serving in Afghanistan. She opened the eye-level oven to check on the potatoes before placing three slices of meat loaf on the heated stovetop griddle. "I'd like you to answer one question for me."

His smile faded. "What is it?"

"Are you seeing someone?"

"No. Why?"

"You seem to have a lot of free time. You've volunteered to spend weekends with me and my nephews, and you just invited me to join you at the Den for Military Monday."

"I manage the business whenever Pop takes off, and that has become more often now that I'm back. I'm also restoring classic cars in my spare time."

Fletcher told Nicole that whenever he'd been granted leave, he'd come back to Wickham Falls to reconnect with his family. Once he was deployed, the visits became more infrequent, which had served to exacerbate his mother's anxiety.

"After I was medically discharged, I stayed with my parents while at the same time looking for a house in The Falls. I've always liked this side of town, but folks that live here aren't willing to sell or move. That's when I discovered the old Hutchinson place was on the market." The neighborhoods in Wickham Falls were reminiscent of many throughout the country where social strata were evidenced by the size of one's home, make and model of car, level of education, and a clear delineation between the professionals, working class and the poor.

Nicole gave him a direct stare. "You got Old Man Hutchinson to sell his place?"

Fletcher chuckled softly. The widowed Korean War veteran's grandfather had built the house and Owen Hutchinson had refused to part with it. Despite many offers above what the house was worth because of the land on which it sat, and the pleas from his grandchildren to sell and come live closer to them.

"One day I drove by and saw him sitting on the porch wearing his uniform. I stopped and over the next couple of hours, we traded war stories while drinking beer. That's when he disclosed that we both had been awarded Purple Hearts and Bronze Stars.

"The conversation changed when I told him I was looking for property in The Falls, but I wasn't having much luck. He said he was willing to sell his house, but only to a disabled war veteran. Being disabled was the deal breaker. I used my GI benefit to purchase the property and had a contractor gut the interior, expand it two thousand square feet, add a second story, a two-car garage and erect another garage that doubles as a body shop."

Nicole smiled. "You had to have some special mojo to get him to give up his house. I remember overhearing folks talk about Mr. Hutchinson's house being deemed unsafe for him to live in, because it looked so shabby from the outside."

"Actually, all it needed was replacement windows and a new coat of paint. There were times when I drove by that I thought the house was going to fall down with him inside. Even though the old man was a hoarder, an engineer had found the house structurally sound."

"How many cars have you restored?" Nicole asked as she lowered the flame under the griddle and turned over the meat loaf.

"Four. Right now, I'm working on a 1953 Studebaker. I've rebuilt the engine, but it's going to take a while to repair the interior and the body."

"What do you do with them once they're completely restored?"

"I sell them to collectors. If you're free this weekend, I'd like you to come over and look at what I'm working on."

Fletcher knew he was getting ahead of himself, but he'd enjoyed spending the morning with Nicole. It was as if they were back in school, where she had been so easy to talk with. There never had been a need for him to be other than who he was—himself. It hadn't been that way with other women.

He had been truthful when she'd asked him if he was seeing someone. He had dated a woman for several months after becoming a civilian, but it had ended as quickly as it had begun. It was only after the split that Fletcher knew he wasn't mentally and/or emotionally ready for a committed relationship. He didn't want a relationship with Nicole as much as he wanted to revive their friendship from before he'd asked her to prom.

"I can't this weekend, but can I have a rain check for the next one?"

"Of course."

Nicole turned and punched several buttons on the microwave. "You can wash up over there." She pointed to a door labeled Bath at the opposite end of the kitchen.

Fletcher walked into the bathroom and washed his hands. The space, decorated in shades of blues and grays, contained a shower stall, vanity and commode. It was his first time in the spacious house where Nicole had grown up with her brother. Like the other homes in the area, there were spacious front lawns and backyards, with enough room for children to play under the watchful supervision of their parents.

He returned to the kitchen to find Nicole had set the table in the breakfast nook with plates, flatware, glasses and serving pieces. A platter with slices of grilled meat loaf, a serving bowl with cabbage and another bowl with oven-baked sweet potato wedges were set out on the table. He took the pitcher filled with ice-cold water from her and filled the glasses. Fletcher waited until she was seated on the cushioned bench before he sat opposite her.

After one bite of the meat loaf, Fletcher realized Nicole wasn't a good cook but an exceptional one. The meat was melt-in-the-mouth tender, the red cabbage perfect with tiny pieces of apple, and the sweet potato wedges were dusted with cinnamon and sea salt.

"Do your nephews know how lucky they are to have an aunt who cooks like this?"

Nicole peered at him over the rim of her water glass. "They haven't complained yet. I try to introduce them to vegetables their mother didn't give them. They're now eating broccoli, asparagus, cabbage, spinach and mushrooms."

Fletcher nodded as he swallowed a mouthful of cabbage. "Good for them. Do they ever eat fast food?"

"Hardly ever. The closest they've come to fast food is what they serve at the Fourth of July celebration. A few times Melissa would take them to the mall and feed them whatever they wanted, which didn't sit too well with Reggie since we grew up eating whatever Mom put on the table."

"Did you get along with your sister-in-law?"

"I did, because I refused to get involved in her disagreements with my brother. It was the same when Reggie complained to me about Melissa. I didn't want to be accused of meddling in their marriage. What about you, Fletcher? Do you get along with your brother and sister-in-law?"

He nodded. "Thankfully I do. My sister is married to a wonderful man, and the same can be said for my brother and his wife. I have to admit I do miss my nieces and nephews."

"When was the last time you saw them?"

"I saw my sister and her kids during the Christmas

break, and my brother and his family earlier this spring. Mom is like a kid in a candy shop when she's around her grandchildren, and is always complaining that she doesn't see them often enough."

"Maybe that will change once you give her a couple of grandbabies."

Fletcher picked up the glass of water and drank half of it. At thirty-five he hadn't felt pressured to marry or to father a child, but had mentally given himself until forty to make that decision. First, he had to find a woman with whom to fall in love enough to propose and, most important, they had to decide whether they wanted to have a family together. He'd met women who had opted not to become mothers, and others who were married and divorced and didn't want to repeat the cycle.

He thought of himself as a traditionalist. He believed in marriage and that children should grow up with two parents. That as a husband and father, he would be responsible for providing for his family and, if and when the time came, make certain they were taken care of financially if he was no longer there for them.

"The operative word is not *when* but *if*, Nikki."

She picked up her napkin and touched it to the corners of her mouth. "You don't want children?"

Fletcher closed his eyes for several seconds. "I want kids, but I'd like to be married first."

Her eyebrows lifted slightly. "I suppose no baby daddy for you," she said, smiling.

He nodded. "Not if I can prevent it. I've never slept with a woman without using protection."

"If more men took your lead, then there wouldn't be so many babies that grow up without having fathers in their lives. My second cousin Tyler, who lives in Baltimore, went to a local college on a full athletic scholarship but had fathered three children by the time he was seventeen. He would complain constantly that his baby mamas were giving him grief because they needed money for diapers and formula. He'd plead with them to wait until he made the pros, because then he would make enough money to take care all his kids, but that fell on deaf ears. He resorted to selling drugs, which got him arrested. He lost everything and they got nada."

"Was he good enough to turn pro?"

Nicole slowly nodded. "The basketball scouts would come to every one of his home games to watch him play. He would score on average at least twenty-eight points a game. And his three-throws were comparable to Steph Curry's. Some of the guys would tell him to wear a condom whenever he slept with a woman, but he refused to listen and it cost him."

"What happened to him after his arrest?" Fletcher asked.

"I don't know. The news of his arrest spread like wildfire around his campus, but no one was willing to openly talk about it because the administration saw it as a black mark on their school."

Fletcher concentrating on eating while staring across the table at Nicole. He'd realized they'd talked about a lot of things, yet Nicole still hadn't revealed that much about herself. And he wondered if she had had a relationship or relationships that had left her wary of a commitment, or if she was so career focused that she wasn't willing to allow a man to share her life.

Despite growing up in Wickham Falls and attending the same schools, Fletcher understood that he and Nicole were worlds apart. Her parents were lawyers.

His father owned and operated his own business and his mother was content in her role as a wife and stay-at-home mother to her three children. He'd disappointed his parents when he hadn't gone to college, yet had redeemed himself in their eyes when he'd become an elite soldier. He had come home to assist in the family business, purchase property and put down roots in the town where he'd been born and raised.

Now, like some of the students with whom he'd graduated, Fletcher had to decide what he wanted for his future. And, if he were truly honest, he could see himself settling down with someone like Nicole and spending the rest of his life with her. However, he knew that wasn't possible because her time in The Falls had an expiration date. He recalled her saying, *I'm not going to get involved with someone and then break it off when I leave next year.*

What she did not know was that he was willing to get involved with her and hopeful he could convince her not to leave. He saw her as a challenge, and there was nothing Fletcher liked better than a challenge, because whenever he played, he played for keeps.

He wiped his mouth with his napkin. "I'm really looking forward to coming tomorrow for dinner and to meet your nephews. And if tomorrow's dinner is anything like today's lunch, then I wouldn't mind stopping by every once in a while to sit at your table."

"You're welcome to come whenever you want. Just call or send me a text to let me know you're coming."

"You may regret those words, Nikki."

She scrunched up her pert nose. "I don't think so, Fletcher."

He stood. "I'll help you clean up, then I'll drive over

to the shop to get a loaner until your SUV is ready. Billy can follow and drive me back."

Nicole also rose. "I really appreciate you helping me out."

"As I said before, folks in The Falls always look out for one another."

Chapter Four

Nicole waved to the bus driver before she closed the door and drove off. She let out a sigh when she noticed Luke dragging his backpack on the ground rather than wearing it on his back. She had explained to him that it was called a backpack for a reason. Daniel followed his younger brother, and it wasn't the first time Nicole noticed him squinting. She made a mental note to set up an appointment to have his eyes checked.

She hugged Luke and then Daniel. "Hi, guys. How was school today?"

"You ask us that every day, Aunt Nikki," Luke said.

Cupping the back of his head, Nicole kissed his sheared scalp. When she'd taken the boys to the barber before the start of the school year, they had insisted on little or no hair. She hadn't wanted them to have shaved heads, so they'd compromised and told the barber to leave just enough to cover their scalps.

Each time she looked at her nephews she was reminded of their late mother. The most distinctive feature was their wide startled eyes that were the color of newly minted pennies. The summer sun had darkened their complexions to a rich mahogany, while they'd grown several inches since she'd begun caring for them.

"I say that because I want to know what you did in class."

"I looked in Luke's room and saw him sitting on the naughty chair next to Miss Harper's desk," Daniel announced proudly.

Luke rounded on his brother. "Why do you always snitch on me, Danny?"

Daniel glared at Luke. "I'm not snitching, Aunt Nikki. Luke was bad again."

Nicole held up her hand. "That's enough, Daniel."

"I wasn't naughty, Auntie," Luke said defensively. "I pushed Colin when he made fun of my missing teeth."

Nicole kissed his forehead. "What did I tell you about using your hands instead of your brain, Luke? You only use your hands when someone assaults you, to protect yourself, otherwise just walk away. There's an old saying about sticks and stones may break my bones but names will never harm me." She wanted to tell Luke that if at six Colin hadn't lost his front teeth he soon would.

Daniel tugged on Nicole's arm. "Daddy told us you used your hands to knock a man down on the ground."

"That's called hand-to-hand combat, Daniel. Soldiers are taught to use their hands to defend themselves in case an enemy attacks them. Enough talk about fighting. After you two change out of your school clothes, I need you to come to the kitchen so we can talk about something." She wanted to tell them about sleepovers with their grandparents every other weekend and Fletcher's potential involvement on their lives.

"Can we have milk and cookies for a snack?" Luke asked.

She smiled. "Of course, you can."

Daniel pointed to the sedan parked in the driveway. "Is that your new car, Aunt Nikki?"

"No. It's a loaner. My car is at a repair shop getting fixed."

"But Othello can't fit in it," Luke whined. The dog, who had been reclining on the porch, stood at the mention of his name.

"That's true," Nicole confirmed, "but I should have my car back in a few days." Fletcher had offered her a Honda Civic for her use until the Pathfinder was repaired. Othello always claimed the SUV's cargo area whenever she took the dog with them during a road trip. "Go inside and change so you can have your snack. Don't forget to—"

"Wash our hands," the boys chorused, laughing.

Nicole hid a knowing grin as she waved at one of her neighbors driving slowly down the street. It was if nothing had changed since she'd left The Falls for college. Fletcher was right when he said folks in her neighborhood weren't willing to sell their homes to anyone; the exception was family members. Once her parents had decided to downsize and retire to a warmer climate, they'd offered Reggie the house as a wedding gift.

She had loved the house where she'd grown up and had looked forward to coming back during college breaks and military leaves. But once her parents had moved to Florida, she hadn't felt comfortable asking Melissa if she could stay with them until her next assignment. Her sister-in-law had become very territorial about *her house* and didn't want outsiders just dropping in to stay. Nicole had held her tongue when she'd wanted to remind Melissa that she wasn't an outsider and that Reggie was her brother.

She had come to look forward to sleeping in her parents' guest bedroom and had grown fond of Miami's vibe and weather and her conversations with her mother about her future in the corps. Elizabeth Campos, or Liz as most of her close friends called her, had suggested she consider becoming a lawyer because she'd spent many summers accompanying her father to witness his courtroom proceedings.

Liz's kernel of an idea took root when Nicole registered for online courses at the California School of Law, Santa Barbara, and passed the FYLSE—first-year law students' exam—with a near-perfect score. She had selected California because it was one of four states that allowed matriculated students from online schools to take the bar in another state.

She felt Othello's nose on her bare ankle and reached down to scratch him behind his ears. "Sorry, but I can't take you for another run because I can't leave the house now that the boys are here." Nicole found herself talking to the strong, agile and intelligent canine as if he understood everything she was saying. "I'll let you out in the back where you can chase your furry friends."

Reggie had fenced in the property after Daniel had begun walking. Melissa would sit out during the warmer weather with her young son to keep an eye on him.

Othello loved chasing any unsuspecting wildlife that ventured onto the property. Most times he'd lie completely still and then pounce. The first time he'd caught a squirrel he'd held it in his mouth, shaking it gently before releasing the frightened rodent. He had been trained to track and capture a target but not kill. She walked around to the side of the house, opened the door to the white PVC gate, and Othello loped through. She closed and locked the gate, then returned to go inside the house.

Nicole watched Daniel and Luke dunk their cookies in the glasses of milk before biting into them. Once a week she baked homemade cookies; this week it was peanut butter shortbread. "I saw Grandpa Clarke today and I told him you can have sleepovers every other weekend."

Luke's eyes grew wider. "Really?"

She smiled. "Yes, really." Nicole knew how much the boys loved hanging out with their first cousins even if it meant sleeping on an air mattress in the small, cramped bedroom.

"When are we going?" Daniel asked.

"This Friday and then the next Friday. That will be the Labor Day weekend, so you can stay over until Monday evening. I told Grandpa that I'll drop you off before six and pick you up on Sundays around six."

The two boys exchanged high fives.

"Aunt Nikki, why can't we go to Grandpa's every weekend because we don't have homework?" Daniel questioned.

"You're going to be with me and my friend, whom you will meet tomorrow. I've invited him to dinner to meet you."

Luke narrowed his eyes. "You have a boyfriend?"

"No, Luke, I don't have a boyfriend."

"Danny has a girlfriend," Luke said in singsong.

"I do not!" Daniel shouted. "Daddy said I couldn't have a girlfriend until I am sixteen."

Nicole rolled her eyes upward. She didn't know when it had happened since they'd returned from Florida, but the brothers seemed unable to stop teasing or tattling on each other. "If you two keep at it, then you're not going anywhere. You will spend every weekend in your rooms reading. Is that what you want?"

"No, Auntie," they said in unison.

Whenever they called her Auntie, she knew they were attempting to diffuse the situation. And despite having them in counseling, the therapist said considering what they'd recently gone through, both boys appeared to be adjusting well now that they'd accepted that their mother and unborn baby sister were with angels in heaven.

Her voice and expression softened when she said, "My friend wants to take you hiking and fishing. He also knows how to make old cars new again." Nicole knew the mention of cars had elicited some excitement when both boys exchanged high fives for the second time. Daniel had admitted he wanted to become a race-car driver, while Luke had exhibited artistic talents when drawing images of the Batmobile. "I invited him to join us for dinner tomorrow, so I expect you to be on your best behavior," Nicole continued.

Daniel's eyes were as round as silver dollars. "Aunt Nikki, will he show us how to fix a car?"

"That's something you will have to ask him."

Daniel asked another question. "Does he race cars?"

"I don't believe he does."

"Will he let me draw pictures of his old cars?"

"If you ask him, Luke, then I'm sure he'll agree."

They continued to bombard Nicole with questions about Fletcher, which she was unable to answer. She was certain once they met him, he would get an earful about what they wanted to do. She sincerely hoped he was ready for her inquisitive and somewhat rambunctious nephews.

"You need to finish your milk and cookies so you can do homework."

"What's for dinner, Aunt Nikki?" Daniel questioned.

"Guacamole, Mexican street corn and tacos." She'd planned to make beef, shrimp and chicken tacos.

Daniel cheered, while Luke got up and did a happy dance. Even though they'd complained about the intense Florida heat and humidity, her nephews had become obsessed with Latin cuisine. Although Nicole had purchased several cookbooks with recipes from Mexico, the Caribbean and Central and South America, the only drawback was finding herbs and spices in rural West Virginia. She'd managed to offset her problem by calling her mother and asking her to overnight mail whatever she'd needed for a recipe. The spice cabinet and a refrigerator drawer contained everything she needed to replicate her favorite dishes.

Fletcher rang the doorbell and then stared down at the toes of his spit-shined boots. He knew he'd shocked his father when he'd informed him that he was leaving early because he had to go home to shave and shower before meeting someone. Jesse Austen had attempted to press him about who he was seeing, but Fletcher had refused to take the bait. His father and all of Wickham Falls would know soon enough that he, Nicole and her nephews would be seen around town together. The Falls had a documented population of less than five thousand living within four square miles and keeping secrets was nearly impossible.

The door opened, his head popped up and he smiled when coming face-to-face with Nicole. She was dressed entirely in black: long-sleeved stretchy top with a pair of matching slacks and ballerina-type flats. The color made her petite frame look even slimmer while the clingy fabric flattered her soft curves.

She opened the door wider. Light from an overhead pendant illuminated the entryway and Nicole's bare face. "Please come in."

Fletcher walked into the entryway. A vase with a colorful bouquet of roses in shades ranging from blood red to pure white sat on the drop-leaf table. "I hope I'm not too early."

"I'm glad you're early because it will give you time to hang out with Daniel and Luke before we sit down to eat. They're watching television in the family room. And thank you for the flowers. They're beautiful."

Fletcher curbed the urge to lean over and kiss her cheek, remembering her warning about getting too close to her when the Belgian Malinois was present. "I wasn't certain whether you'd like them." He'd called the local florist and had them deliver a bouquet of flowers as a house gift.

"I'm not ashamed to admit that I have a weakness for flowers and scented candles."

"Are you admitting that you're a romantic?"

She affected a mischievous grin. "No comment."

"Yeah, you are," he countered, smiling. Knowing she was a romantic would make it easier for them to have an uncomplicated liaison. He already knew she wasn't interested in a romantic entanglement and having her nephews as buffers was certain to make it easy for them to remain friends.

Nicole leaned closer, but not so close to touch him as Othello watched their every motion. “I told Daniel and Luke you were into cars,” she whispered like a co-conspirator, “so get ready for the inquisition. And, by the way, you can take off your jacket. Dinners here are very informal.”

Fletcher shrugged out of the black jacket he had paired with matching slacks, set it on a straight-backed chair and then squared his shoulders. “I’m ready.” He followed Nicole through the living and dining rooms into a spacious area that doubled as the family room. A large wall-mounted television was tuned to a channel showing cartoons.

“Daniel, Luke, we have company,” Nicole announced softly. The two boys popped up from a floral love seat. “I’d like to you to meet Mr. Fletcher. Fletcher, these are my nephews, Luke and Daniel.”

The taller of the two approached Fletcher and held out his hand. “I’m Danny. And it’s nice to meet you, Mr. Fletcher.”

Fletcher took the extended hand and shook it, all the while keeping a wary eye on Othello. “It’s just Fletcher. And it’s a pleasure to meet you, too, Danny.”

Luke, who hadn’t been able to stop staring up at Fletcher, was suddenly propelled into action, offering his hand. “I’m Luke. Aunt Nikki said you have a lot of cars.”

Fletcher nodded. “What she probably meant was that I work on a lot of cars.”

Daniel pushed out his lower lip. “You don’t have a car?”

“Oh, I have a car,” he admitted. “In fact, I have several cars." Fletcher gave Nicole a barely perceptible wink after she'd picked up the remote device and turned off the television. "Let's sit down and I'll tell you all about them." He walked over to the sofa and sat as the brothers flanked him. Othello lay down less than a foot away, his muzzle resting on both paws, watching him intently.

Nicole returned to the kitchen to put the finishing touches on dinner, confident that Fletcher would keep her charges thoroughly entertained when talking about cars. She knew where the fascination had come from, because it had been the same with her brother. For as long as she could remember Reggie had had a Matchbox car collection. And like most boys she'd grown up with, he'd treated his first car, which for most boys his age were hoopties, like a top-of-the-line luxury vehicle.

She was thirteen and her brother sixteen when she'd accompanied Reggie across town to Fletcher's father's garage to have him look at his 1986 Plymouth Reliant because it needed a new muffler.

Although she and Fletcher had been the same age and attended the same school, she'd rarely spoken to him, but that day was the first time he'd openly acknowledged her by name. She'd been so awestruck that one of the cutest boys in middle school had spoken directly to her, all she could do was nod. It was later that night in her bedroom that she'd pounded the mattress so hard, chiding herself for reacting like a complete dunce when presented with the perfect opportunity to engage in a conversation with him. She was finally able to vent her frustration when detailing the event in her diary.

Nicole had found herself mooning over Fletcher for years until they reached high school and she saw girls openly flirting to get him to notice them. Once he was selected to join the football team and became an athletic standout, her teenage crush had shattered completely when rumors circulated that he was sleeping with several of the cheerleaders. And knowing the girls were sleeping with him, along with some of the other boys on the team, made Fletcher abhorrent to Nicole. Even when they'd worked together on the senior committees, she'd related to him as a fellow student and nothing more. Fast-forward seventeen years and they were now different people at a different time in their lives.

Fletcher had bought property and planned to spend the rest of his life in The Falls, while she had an expiration date on her tenure. What she had promised herself was to enjoy whatever time she and Fletcher had together during the interim. When she returned to Miami, it would be to pick up the pieces of her life and solidify her future.

Nicole opened the oven and peered at the turkey. She'd called the local butcher and requested a small, fresh turkey. Fortunately, he'd had one on hand and, after leaving the office, she'd stopped by the supermarket to pick up the ingredients she needed for corn bread–sage stuffing. Once the turkey was done, she would finish it off with a fruity brown-sugar glaze. She had decided on side dishes of wilted garlic spinach and caramelized baby carrots rather than her nephews' plea to make mac and cheese. It wasn't easy cooking for children who eschewed vegetables, but Nicole tried, with much success, to introduce them to as many as she could.

The digital thermometer inserted in the thigh of the turkey registered the temperature for doneness. She removed the Thermo-Clad roaster from the oven and set it on a trivet to allow the juices from the turkey to settle. She covered it with the glaze before she placed a pan of Parker House rolls in the oven. Since becoming a temporary guardian for her nephews, Nicole had developed a healthy respect for working mothers, who, in her eyes, were superwomen.

"Do you need help with anything?"

She turned to find that Fletcher had entered the kitchen without her hearing him. He had rolled back the cuffs on the untucked pale blue shirt. "After the turkey rests and I carve it, you can bring it into the dining room. Did you answer all their questions about cars?"

"Most of them. They claim they want to help me restore the Studebaker."

Nicole gave him a skeptical look. "Do you think that's wise?"

"You'll see when you bring them over to the house. Just make certain y'all wear something you won't mind getting soiled with grease and oil."

"I'll definitely keep that in mind," she said.

"I like your nephews. They're very bright *and* inquisitive."

"I like them, too," Nicole said in agreement. "Even though they may look a lot alike, they have very different personalities. You'll discover Daniel is rather laid-back, while Luke is more outgoing and has a quick temper. Reggie always had to put him in time-out or ground him whenever he acted out."

Reggie making her an aunt was one of the milestones in her life; she'd told him as "Auntie Nikki" her sole focus was to spoil them. Once she was a civilian, she returned to The Falls to visit with them or driven up to take the boys back to Miami to reconnect with their paternal grandparents. Before she'd become an aunt, Nicole hadn't thought of herself as maternal, but now that she was a guardian for Daniel and Luke, she'd felt the pull of motherhood for the first time.

She had been forthcoming when Fletcher had asked when she was going to become a mother. Nicole wanted to follow in the footsteps of her mother and find a man with whom she could fall in love, marry and share their children. At thirty-five, she knew her biological clock was ticking and, with each subsequent year, it would tick louder and faster, but she did remind herself that she had an option: adoption.

However, her priority wasn't a relationship, marriage or even motherhood. It was seeing to the physical and emotional well-being of her nephews until their father completed treatment. The most important thing on her agenda when she moved back to Miami was to secure another position with a law firm—a firm where she did not have to work fifty to sixty hours to make the billing quota.

"Luke needs to be involved in a competitive sport like karate or judo," Fletcher suggested. "It will build his confidence, instill discipline while allowing him to release some of his aggression."

"I could teach him Katame-waza, but I don't think he would appreciate his aunt holding him down until he submits."

Fletcher's eyebrows shot up in surprise. "You know Katame-waza?"

"Yes. I'm a student of marital arts. It helps me to focus and release stress. I'd just begun kickboxing lessons before I came here."

"Forget what I said about throwing you up in the air like a beach ball."

Nicole flashed a wide grin. "Not to worry, Fletcher. You're safe around me."

"That's reassuring to know." Fletcher sucked in an audible breath. "I smell bread."

"I put up dough last night for Parker House rolls."

"Hot damn," Fletcher crooned, grinning from ear to ear. "I can't believe we're having Thanksgiving in August."

Nicole's grin matched his. "I always believe in treating my guests to the best."

Fletcher's smile vanished quickly. "Am I a guest or a friend, Nicole?"

She gave him a direct stare. "You're both. The first time you eat in my home, you're a guest."

A sixth sense told Nicole that Fletcher wanted to be more than a friend. She'd been exposed to, and was always the minority when it came to men once she'd joined the Naval Reserve Officers Training Corps, and she was more than aware when a man was interested in her for more than friendship. She'd had two serious relationships and, while neither had lasted more than a year, they had made her wary of the opposite sex.

Nicole probably would have considered becoming a friend with benefits when it came to Fletcher if she wasn't returning to Miami. She'd admitted to him that she was a romantic—one that always allowed her heart to overrule her head. Sleeping with Fletcher and having to leave him would negatively affect her emotionally. She shook her head as if to dismiss the notion of getting romantically involved with him.

Chapter Five

"I don't see you for weeks and now that you're here, I feel as if I'm talking to myself."

Fletcher had come over after the garage closed to have dinner with his parents. He'd helped his mother clean up the kitchen before they'd retreated to the family room to watch television with his father. Once Jesse retired for bed, Carla had suggested they sit on the back porch and relax in what had become an Austen family tradition.

As children Fletcher and his siblings would gather on the porch to play board and/or video games while their parents watched their antics. It was what Carla called "quality family time." The exception was during the school week because of homework. As they got older, even Fridays and Saturdays became the exception. But Sunday evenings were special and Fletcher had never tired of sitting on the porch with his family, catching up on what was going on in their lives.

Stretching out his legs and crossing his feet at the ankles, Fletcher smiled at his mother. He always enjoyed sitting on the screened-in back porch and watching the sun set as he'd done as a child.

Carla Murphy Austen had given up a career as a social worker when she'd married his father to become a stay-at-home mother after giving birth to three children barely eighteen months apart. One child was barely toilet trained before she'd had another one in diapers. She would celebrate her sixtieth birthday in December, yet could pass for a woman in her early fifties. Although she had begun graying in her midtwenties, Carla refused to dye her hair and the short curly strands were now a shimmering silver. The color was the perfect complement to her flawless brown complexion with its orange undertones.

"I was being polite and didn't want to interrupt you." His mother had launched into a monologue about what was going on in the lives of her grandchildren, who, come winter, were going to take ice-skating lessons. She'd recently visited his sister in Ann Arbor, Michigan, where Charlene and her husband taught English and American history respectively, at the University of Michigan.

Twin dimples dotted Carla's smooth cheeks when she pressed her lips together. "I don't know why you think I don't know when something is bothering my children after all these years. You become a mute, Charlene resorts to waterworks and Sean throws things. Now, tell me what's on your mind."

"There's nothing on my mind, Mom," he lied smoothly.

There was a lot on his mind and it all had to do with Nicole Campos. It had been nearly two weeks since he'd shared dinner at her house with her and her nephews; everything about that night lingered around the fringes of his memory when he least expected. Other than his own family, it was the first time he'd felt like part of a family unit where he had imagined Nicole as his wife and Danny and Luke their sons.

Fletcher had had more than his share of women—a few he'd slept with and many more that were friends willing to spend hours talking, playing cards or watching sports. He still had to figure out what he wanted with Nicole.

Whenever they were alone, he'd found her guarded, more a military officer than a civilian. However, when she was with her nephews, the transformation was startling. Her expression softened, as did her voice. She was quick to laugh at something they'd said, while he measured every word because he didn't want to say something that would make her put up the invisible wall, treating him as if he did not exist as she'd done seventeen years before.

"Are you sure, Fletcher? You look as if you've lost your best friend."

He forced a smile. "I'm sure."

There was another prolonged silence until Carla said, "Your father told me he noticed the change in you a couple of weeks ago. Are you in pain? Or are you experiencing PTSD?"

"No to both questions." When hospitalized he'd had a number of sessions with an army psychiatrist to talk about what he'd experienced when deployed. The only time he'd requested pain meds was post-op.

Now, whenever he experienced discomfort, he elevated his leg, applied ice and then moist heat to the damaged limb.

"If it's not your leg, then it has to be something to do with the judge's daughter. Jesse told me you spent a lot of time with her after her car broke down. I know you liked her when you were in high school. Should I assume your feelings for her haven't changed?"

"I didn't know your husband was a gossiper."

"Jesse is not a gossiper," Carla said defensively. "He just mentioned it to me in passing."

Fletcher wanted to tell his mother that his father talked too much, but knew she would defend her husband of nearly forty years to the death. "Does he tell you about every customer who comes into the garage to have their vehicle serviced?"

Carla managed to look embarrassed when she averted her eyes. "No, but he thought it strange that after you arranged to have her car towed to the garage you didn't come back until hours later."

Fletcher knew if he didn't tell his mother about his agreement with Nicole, she would find out soon enough once they were seen in public together. "I will be seeing Nicole off-and-on while she's in The Falls taking caring of her nephews."

He related everything that had happened in the courtroom: Nicole's compromise with her brother's in-laws and his offer to stand in as a male role model for her nephews until their father's return.

"So, there's nothing romantic going on between you and her?" Carla questioned.

"No, Mom. Nikki and I were friends in high school and we're still friends."

Carla rocked back and forth on the cushioned rocker. “Do you want more than friendship, son?”

His mother was asking something he’d asked himself since coming face-to-face with Nicole again. Adolescent feelings had been replaced with adult emotions and the difference between the two was like night and day.

As a high school student, Nicole was poised and seemingly much too sophisticated for someone that young and confident. She’d attended most of the school’s football, basketball and baseball home games though she’d refused to join the other students for the victory rallies.

“It’s not about what I want, Mom. Nicole is only going to be in The Falls until the beginning of next year, and she’s already said she doesn’t plan to get involved with anyone during this time.”

“You did not answer my question, son. Maybe I should’ve asked if you could possibly see Nicole as a potential wife. My mother always told me whenever I agreed to date a man, I should always view him as a potential husband. If not, then I shouldn’t waste my or his time.”

Fletcher shifted on his chair. “Times were very different when you and Grandpa were dating. There was a lot of pressure for girls to marry, but nowadays women have options.”

“I know I’m jumping the gun, but has Nicole told you she doesn’t want to marry or have children?”

Fletcher was becoming annoyed with his mother’s line of questioning. He had seen Nicole twice and it wasn’t as if they’d pledged their undying love for each other. It wasn’t until after their dinner that he’d felt as if she had truly forgiven him for the acerbic words he'd used to offset her rejection.

"Do you mind if we change the topic? Nothing is going to come of it."

"Is that what you want?" Carla asked.

"It's what I'd like at this time," Fletcher said, softening his tone. He didn't like verbally sparring with his mother, but there were occasions when she was like a dog with a bone and refused to stop questioning him until he was forced to excuse himself and leave.

Fletcher knew his mother had always been overly concerned about her firstborn. She'd been visibly upset when he'd announced he was going to reject several athletic scholarships to enlist in the army. She'd been inconsolable when he'd told her he was to be deployed. After his first placement, she'd seemed to accept that he was going to be a career officer; his subsequent deployments were less and less emotional.

Pushing to his feet, he leaned over and kissed his mother's cheek. "Thanks for dinner. I promise to come more often."

Carla rested a hand on his stubble. "I know you're busy at the garage and working on your cars, so don't feel obligated to come and see me."

Fletcher kissed her again. "Stop with the guilt trip, Mom. I used to come by so often that you got tired of seeing me."

"I never get tired of seeing my children. And now that Sean and Charlene live in other states, I've become somewhat clingy when it comes to you."

Cupping her elbow, Fletcher helped Carla to stand. He held her close, resting his chin on the top of her head. "I love you, Mom, and I don't want you to worry about me."

"As a mother I have a right to worry about my children. You'll realize this once you have children of your own."

Fletcher wanted to tell his mother that if or when he did become a father, he planned to raise his children to become independent adults able to make rational decisions for themselves. Carla was affectionate and nurturing, but she was also overly protective of her children and grandchildren. When he revealed to his parents that he'd negotiated purchasing the Hutchinson property, Carla had happily announced that now that he was going to permanently live in The Falls, she could look forward to him marrying and giving her more grandchildren.

"It's late. Pop's in bed and so should you be. Come walk me to the door and lock it after me." They left the porch and walked to the front of the house.

"Are you going to any cookouts over the holiday weekend?" Clara asked.

"Nah. Do you and Pop plan to cook out?"

"Not really," she admitted. "I'm trying to convince him to cut back his hours this week so we can drive down to Texas to see Sean and the kids."

"Do you want me to help you out and suggest Pop take at least a couple of weeks off and take you away?"

"Would you please, Fletcher?"

"Of course, Mom. He knows by now that the place will not fall apart if he's not there." It wouldn't be the first time he would advocate on his mother's behalf to convince his father to take time off and spend time with her.

Going on tiptoe, Carla kissed his chin. "Thank you."

He waited until he heard the distinctive click of the lock to the front door slide into place before he walked to his car. Tapping the start-engine button, Fletcher shifted into Reverse and backed out of the driveway. He lived less than half a mile from his parents' house. There were times when he'd walked the distance, but not tonight. He had put in a full day at the garage because one of their part-time mechanics had had a family emergency.

Fletcher knew he would eventually assume full responsibility for operating the business, and had taken steps to ensure its viability. Newer cars had electronic components and he had recommended his father purchase a computer to diagnose mechanical problems. Initially, Jesse had balked at the cost of the computer, so rather than get into an argument with his father, Fletcher had purchased it, using his own money. The transaction had caused a temporary rift between father and son. Jesse had claimed he did not need his son using his personal funds for the business. The hostility finally deescalated when Fletcher agreed to let his father pay him back in twelve monthly increments.

Not only had he taken advantage of GI benefits when it came to purchasing a house, he'd also used his educational allowance to enroll in an online college, earning an undergraduate degree in business.

Fiscally conservative, Fletcher had invested his deployment bonuses in a retirement account along with the proceeds he earned from selling restored cars to various collectors. His go-between had contacts with owners of junkyards as far away as Kentucky and Tennessee looking for shells of old cars, many of which had rusted away in driveways or backyards for decades. The man arranged for the owners to receive a nominal fee to remove the cars from their property and paid the junk-yard owner a fee based on the condition of the abandoned vehicles.

Fletcher maneuvered into the driveway to his house, pressed the remote attached to the visor and watched the garage door smoothly slide up. He pulled into the empty space next to the GMC Acadia, shut off the engine and got out of the low-slung sports car.

Minutes later, he climbed the staircase to his second-story bedroom. Fletcher looked forward to having weekends to himself—this weekend in particular because it was a long one and he would get to see Nicole again at the Wolf Den for Military Mondays.

Nicole's head popped up when she heard someone knock on the closed door to her office. "Come in. What is it?" she asked Marlena Pratt, the firm's receptionist as she stuck her head through the slight opening.

"I didn't want to call you because I didn't want the walk-in to overhear our conversation."

Suddenly her curiosity was piqued. The firm's practice was to announce the client's arrival before escorting them to the respective office. "Who is it, Miss Pratt?"

"Sasha Manning-Richards."

Nicole went completely still. "Are you talking about Sasha Manning from The Falls?" A wide smile lifted the corners of her mouth.

The middle-aged receptionist with a '60s beehive hairstyle nodded. Marlena was a permanent fixture at the firm, her tenure spanning nearly fifty years. Preston claimed she was the eyes, ears and heartbeat of the office. Although she occasionally forgot to enter an appointment in the computer's calendar, he refused to let her go.

"Please send her in. No, forget it, Miss Pratt. I'll come out to see her," Nicole said quickly. She was anxious to meet the local young woman who'd become a celebrity chef after winning third place in a televised cupcake competition. Sasha had made headlines again when she'd married an up-and-coming country singer.

Nicole left her office and walked down the carpeted hallway to the reception area. The woman standing before her looked nothing like the photographs she had seen of a laughing or smiling Sasha, or how she remembered Sasha before Nicole left The Falls to attend college. The chef was above average height and rail thin. Her hair was a lot darker than the flaming red from her childhood and Nicole wondered if she had taken to dying it.

Smiling, she extended both hands. "How are you, Sasha?"

The startled look in the dark green eyes indicated she hadn't been prepared to see her. Sasha grasped her hands and Nicole was shocked by their iciness. Sasha affected what passed for a smile when her lips barely parted. "I'm better now that I'm back home. When I called to talk to a lawyer, I never would've expected you to be working here."

"Come. We'll talk in my office. Would you like something to drink?"

Sasha shook her head. "Thank you, but I'm good."

Normally, Nicole would have taken a client into the conference room, but judging from Sasha's uneasiness, she felt the chef would feel more comfortable in a less formal space. Nicole pointed to a chair at a small round table in the corner. "Please sit down." Waiting until Sasha was seated, Nicole took a chair opposite her. "When did you get back to The Falls?"

"Last night. I should be asking you the same thing. When did you come back to work for Preston McAvoy?"

Nicole laced her fingers on the table. "I'm here on a temporary basis."

"The last I heard you were an officer in the Marines."

"I was an officer. I gave the corps fifteen years, and I'm now a civilian lawyer." She leaned forward. "Now, tell me why you're here." Within seconds Nicole had shifted into professional mode.

She listened intently, purposefully not showing any emotion when Sasha gave her an overview of her life since she'd enrolled in culinary school to become a pastry chef. Sasha had been totally unprepared to become a celebrity, and even more so to marry a man with superstar status. She had even put her career on hold to tour with him.

"To the public we were the redhead and the cowboy, but no one had any idea that Wes set out to control my career once it eclipsed his. After a while I'd had enough and decided to file for divorce. I dropped my married name, so I'm now legally Sasha Manning, and I want to open a bakeshop here in The Falls. What I want is for you to help me set up a corporation for the business."

"Do you have a location for your business?"

"Yes. When I told my mother what I wanted to do, she told me that the trophy shop had closed a few months back and that it's still vacant. I had her call the Realtor and give her a check for at least three months to hold the space for me."

"You'll also have to contact the building department to get the necessary permits to install whatever equipment you need to become operational," Nicole reminded her.

"I know," Sasha confirmed. "I figured it shouldn't take more than three months to get approval for the corporation and a determination from the town to operate the bakeshop."

Nicole leaned back in her chair. "Setting up the corporation shouldn't take that long, but what I need from you is at least three or four names to submit to the state so they can run a search."

Reaching into her handbag, Sasha unfolded a sheet of paper and handed it to Nicole. "I've written down five in the order of preference. What I'm certain of is what I plan to call the business. Sasha's Sweet Shoppe. That's *shop* with two *p*'s and an *e*."

"I like it."

Sasha flashed a warm, open smile for the first time. "I never thought when I left The Falls that I would come back to start over. The only thing I'd thought about when growing up was leaving because I felt as if I was being smothered." She took out her checkbook. "Please tell me what I owe you."

Nicole stood. "Miss Pratt will go over the fees with you after I tell her what we discussed. You can also leave your contact information with her, and as soon as I get the final word on your corporation, I'll call you."

Sasha also rose to her feet. "Thanks so much, Nicole."

She smiled. "Welcome home."

The chef returned her smile. "It's good to be home."

Nicole waited for Sasha to leave the office before she returned to the files on her desk. She had put an appreciable dent in the number of client files covering the surface of the credenza in her office.

She spied the sticky note on her planner: Military Para for Monday. It had been nearly two weeks since she'd last seen Fletcher and she was looking forward to seeing him again and connecting with former and active military at the Wolf Den.

Nicole skipped down the porch at the same time Fletcher drove up in a classic blue Chevrolet Corvette convertible. He came to a stop, leaned over and opened the passenger-side door. She slipped onto the leather seat, fastened the seat belt and then turned to stare at his long-sleeved black T-shirt stamped with US Army across the chest, black jeans and military-issue sand-colored boots.

"Hi." Her eyes met Fletcher's when he removed his sunglasses. He'd sent a text earlier that morning to indicate he planned to arrive at her house at three.

He pointed to the bars on the cap identifying her rank. "Hi, yourself. Should I salute you now or later, Captain Campos?"

"There will be no saluting tonight," she said, smiling.

"You think not," Fletcher said under his breath. "Once everyone gets a look at that cap, there will be a lot of saluting."

"Should I take it off?"

"No way. You look very cute."

Nicole had changed several times before selecting a pair of tan cropped pants and matching running shoes with a navy T-shirt with USMC over her heart. Her keys, driver's license and cell phone were in the leather wristlet on her arm. She shyly lowered her eyes with his compliment.

"Thank you."

Nicole wanted to believe that the two-week separation and her busy schedule had been enough for her not to dwell on the man sitting so close to her. Even with her nephews spending every other weekend with their grandparents, her days and nights had been filled with catching up on laundry, ironing, cleaning every room in the house and visiting the supermarket to replenish the pantry and restock the refrigerator.

During her downtime she'd attempted to catch up on one or two of her favorite television shows, but usually fell asleep before the episodes ended. After a while she wasn't certain whether she was pushing herself too hard not to think about the man whose presence affected her more than she was willing to acknowledge.

She had been unable to keep her eyes off Fletcher when seated across the dining room table from him the night she'd introduced him to her nephews. Not only did he have impeccable table manners, she discovered he was a wonderful conversationalist. He'd kept both boys equally entertained with stories about hiking in the mountains with his father and younger brother. And whenever they went fishing, they would come home with a large enough catch for four Friday-night fish fries. Daniel and Luke had held on to every word and then said they couldn't wait to go fishing with Uncle Fletcher. Nicole had been just as surprised when they called him Uncle as Fletcher was, and he'd held up his hand to indicate for her to let it go when she opened her mouth to correct them. She had introduced him as "Mr." not "Uncle" Fletcher.

"How old is this beauty?" she asked as Fletcher executed a smooth turn and reversed direction.

"Older than both of us. It debuted in 1953 at the GM Motorama Show and production began later that year. All the cars were white, which led to flat sales. But the company refused to give up. The next year, more colors were made available and the car got a power boost. And what makes it even more unique is the world's first production car to be made out of glass fiber. It was a daring move, but it worked."

Nicole felt the power of the sports car as it accelerated. "Did you restore this car?"

"No. I got it in a barter. I'd restored a 1957 Ford Thunderbird for a collector and he gave me this Blue Flame Special because his preference is classic Fords. I did add seat belts as a safety precaution."

"How fast have you pushed this beauty?"

"I got her up to a hundred and thirty before easing off."

"Where were you that you could go that fast?"

Fletcher smiled. "The guy I got her from has a track on his property, where he races his cars."

"He's a collector with a racetrack." Nicole's query was a statement.

"He's worth millions and cars are what he calls his guilty pleasure. Some men collect fine art, boats, planes, priceless jewels, and others cars."

"Don't forget women," she interjected.

Throwing back his head, Fletcher laughed loudly. "Women. Can't live with them and can't live without them."

"Is that why you're not married, Fletcher? Because you can't live with a woman?"

He sobered quickly. "The truth is they can't live with me. I don't know what it is, but I seem to attract needy women who demand too much of my time."

"Perhaps it's because they look at you as their rescuer and are afraid if you're not around they won't be protected."

Fletcher slowed as he approached the railroad tracks running through the middle of town, looked both ways and then drove across. "Why would you say that?"

"Whether you realize it or not, you're a modern-day superhero. Not only did you offer to drive me to the courthouse, you also volunteered to step in as a mentor for my nephews—although I had the law on my side because I'd filed the necessary documents with the court allowing me custodial protection for my brother's children."

Fletcher was silent for several minutes as he pondered Nicole's assessment of his behavior. As the eldest of his parents' three children, he'd been raised to always look out for his younger siblings—his sister in particular. He'd lost track of the number of times Charlene would threaten to get her big brother to take care of a situation she'd gotten herself into and, because he wasn't unable to deal with her tears, he had. Fletcher had always been tall for his age, and his height was enough to intimidate those looking for a physical altercation. Once he'd joined the military, he'd dated women who'd wanted him to protect them from ex-boyfriends or to help them get out of a toxic relationship. By that time his body had filled out and he'd put on a lot of muscle from the rigorous training to become a Special Forces medical sergeant. He was able to stay in peak condition to parachute, swim and scuba dive.

"I've never thought of myself in that way," he admitted.

"Well, you should, Captain America," Nicole teased. "And the next time you look for a girlfriend, you should pick one who has a life of her own."

"Are you applying for the position? Because you do have a life—and no doubt a very busy one."

"I'm sorry, but I have to disqualify myself."

"Why, Nikki?"

"Because I can't be here for the long run."

"Do you place an expiration date on all your relationships?"

"No. Just this one if we were to begin dating each other."

Fletcher's grin was so wide he was certain Nicole could see his molars. "I'm not opposed to a relationship of short duration, if you're amenable."

Nicole stared straight ahead. "It really wouldn't bother you if we broke up after four or five months?"

"I'm not going to say it wouldn't bother me, because when I date a woman, I'm usually all in. But in this case you're the one in the driver's seat."

"Okay," she said after what appeared to be an interminable pause. "I'll see you whenever I can, because of Daniel and Luke, but I want to warn you that when it comes time for me to leave The Falls, I want a clean break."

He resisted the urge to pump his fist in victory. He hadn't expected Nicole to agree to date him, and he was willing to accept whatever time they would have together.

Fletcher signaled and turned off onto the local road leading to the Wolf Den. He managed to find one of the few remaining spaces in the parking lot, shut down the engine and raised the convertible's top. Unbuckling his seat belt, he leaned over and brushed his mouth across Nicole's parted lips. Her intake of breath indicated he'd shocked her.

"You've got yourself a deal," he whispered. Fletcher got out of the Corvette and came around to help Nicole out. Holding on to her hand, he led her around to the front door to the eating establishment with the reputation of serving some of the best barbecue in the county.

Chapter Six

Nicole wondered if she had been caught in a trap of her own choosing when she walked into the Den with Fletcher's arm around her waist. Once her eyes adjusted to coming out of the brilliant sunlight, she saw a small crowd of men and a few women in military paraphernalia staring at her.

"Oorah!" echoed throughout the restaurant as fellow marines greeted her, some with first bumps and others with salutes.

"What can I get the captain?" shouted one of the two bartenders serving drinks to those standing two-deep at the bar.

Fletcher pulled Nicole closer. "What's your poison?"

She smiled up at him. He had removed his sunglasses and she found herself drowning in the amber orbs. "Whatever beer is on tap." Nicole preferred wine, but the occasion called for beer and other spirits.

Fletcher held up two fingers. "Two beers, and put them on my tab."

It had been a long time since Nicole had been inside the legendary pub/sports bar, as the familiar aromas of barbecue and smoked meats wafted to her nostrils. Most young people waited patiently to reach legal drinking age to visit the Wolf Den, because it was the only business in The Falls with a liquor license. The owners were vigilant and had a no-nonsense policy about serving alcohol to minors. They checked IDs of everyone under thirty and that included military personnel.

She'd rarely hung out with other students and when she had it was at Ruthie's—a family-style restaurant with an all-you-can-eat buffet.

Fletcher pressed his mouth to her ear. "Let me see if I can find a table before I bring you your beer and put in an order before the kitchen gets too busy." She followed him as he shouldered his way through the throng of men and women excitedly talking to one another and loudly greeting newcomers. Fletcher found an empty booth and seated her. He winked at her. "Don't run away. I'll be right back."

Nicole stared at his broad shoulders under the black T-shirt as he walked. She had no intention of running away now that she'd agreed to go out with him. She knew their relationship would not be traditional in nature because of her schedule and the responsibility of caring for her nephews. The only time she and Fletcher would be able to see each other alone would be the weekends the boys stayed with their grandparents. She had laid the ground rules for their relationship and hopefully Fletcher would not attempt to break or thwart them.

It had been more than a year since she had had anything that resembled a social life. Joining the other associates for dinner, or going to a local club after a hectic workweek to let off a little steam, had been the extent of what passed as fun. One of the partners had asked her out under the guise he'd wanted to discuss her future with the firm, but Nicole had seen through his subterfuge when he'd reached across the table to hold her hand. Not only was he her boss, he was also married, and she'd had no intention of carrying on an affair with a married man.

Dating Fletcher was safe. He was part owner in a family business, and now that he'd purchased a house, he planned to spend the rest of his life in Wickham Falls. Like in many small towns, one's reputation was valued above all else. Besmirching a good reputation usually led to ostracism and exclusion. She'd realized this when he'd talked about not wanting to become an unwed father.

Well, she mused, she wasn't ready to start a family of her own when her life was still in flux. Although she'd paid the maintenance fee on her condo six months in advance and was solvent, she still had to look for a position with another Miami law firm. Once she'd revealed to her parents that she wanted to follow in their steps and become a lawyer, Nicole had teased her father that she did not want to begin her career as a prosecutor as he had, but preferred working in a firm.

"I didn't expect to see you here, Captain Campos."

Nicole's head popped up when she heard a deep, familiar voice. She half rose from her seat and smiled at a tall, slender man with refined features in a face the color of polished mahogany. "I thought I'd surprise everyone and show up, Major Adams." Former active army for a decade, the dentist was now a reservist. Three years her senior, Dwight and her brother, Reggie, had always been thick as thieves. Both friends had married local girls, but Dwight's marriage had ended after less than three years when his wife opposed him setting up a practice in The Falls.

Dwight sat opposite her. "Are you here alone?"

She shook her head. "No. I came with Fletcher Austen."

Dwight's inky black eyebrows shot up. "You and Fletcher?"

Nicole nodded, smiling. "Yes. Me and Fletcher." Now that she had agreed to date him, she was willing to openly acknowledge that she and Fletcher were a couple. She couldn't tell by Dwight's impassive expression how he felt about his best friend's sister.

"How's Reggie doing?"

"I'm not sure. The treatment center has very strict rules about outside contact until he completes his first three months."

Dwight ran a hand over his shaved scalp. "I really miss hanging out with my buddy during the off-season."

Nicole flashed a small smile. "Once he completes treatment and comes home, you guys will pick up where you left off."

"Did your brother tell you that I've volunteered to be his sponsor once he completes treatment?"

Nicole nodded. "He did mention it."

She knew her parents wanted their son to move to Florida and had offered to look after their grandchildren until Reggie was able to secure a position with a local college. Whether in The Falls or in Miami, her brother would have the safety net needed to keep his new life on track.

“Hey, Doc, what’s up?” Fletcher said as he placed two mugs of frothy beer on the table.

Dwight stood and gave Fletcher a strong embrace. “I was just keeping your girlfriend occupied to stop some of these knuckleheads from hitting on her.”

Fletcher rested a hand on Dwight’s shoulder. “Thanks, man.”

The dentist winked at Nicole. “I’ll see you again when you bring your nephews in for their next checkup.”

“Of course.” Nicole had taken the boys in for a checkup and cleaning in June. Their upcoming appointment was scheduled a week before Christmas.

Fletcher waited for Dwight to walk away and then sat opposite Nicole. “Were dudes trying to hit on you?”

“No. Dwight is just pulling your leg.”

“That’s good, because I don’t want to have to turn the Den out when I thump some dude for disrespecting my lady.”

“If you start a barroom fight, I’ll never talk to you again,” Nicole said.

Fletcher chuckled. “I was just pulling your leg,” he countered, smiling. “I hope you don’t mind that I ordered ribs, chicken and brisket with a couple of sides.”

She waved a hand. “You don’t have to ask. All I had this morning was a cup of coffee and a slice of peanut-buttered toast because I knew I was coming here.”

Fletcher touched his mug to Nicole’s. “If all I had was coffee and toast for breakfast, I’d be as hangry as a bear coming out of hibernation.” He glanced up when he saw the waitress with a tray on her shoulder coming their way. "I think our food is here."

"Yo, Austen," someone called out. "How did you get your order before the rest of us?"

Smiling, Fletcher pointed to Nicole. "Rank does have its privileges."

The young, freckle-faced corporal stood at attention and executed a snappy salute. "Sorry about that, Captain."

Nicole returned the salute and bit back a grin. "I'm glad I came because I like the fact that officers and noncoms can fraternize without the threat of facing a court-martial."

Slumping back in the booth, Fletcher stared at Nicole over the rim of his mug as he took a long swallow. Suddenly he recalled their conversation about her being in love with a man that wasn't an officer and wondered if Nicole was a woman who was willing to sacrifice love in lieu of a career.

"That can only happen in a civilian setting," he said as the waitress set out mouthwatering platters and bowls filled with meat and veggies.

"May I serve you?" Fletcher asked Nicole.

"Please."

He'd just filled a plate for Nicole with barbecued ribs, slices of fork-tender brisket, black-eyed peas and potato salad when Seth Collier sat next to him. "I'm sorry to intrude on you good folks but, Fletcher, I'd like to ask you something."

Fletcher stared at the sheriff of Wickham Falls. He'd exchanged his official uniform for a USMC sweatshirt. "Ask away."

"I know you work for your father, but would you be

willing to work one night a week as an on-call EMT? We're down one man who tripped over his kid's bike and broke his foot. The other two are working twelve-hour shifts to cover for him until he returns. But they're complaining about needing at least one night off a week. I'm only asking you because of your medical training."

"Won't I have to be certified as an EMT?" Fletcher asked.

"You're trained in first-response trauma medicine, which makes you qualified to fill in for Charlie Robinson. His orthopedist predicts he should be medically clear to return to work in another month. I've talked to the mayor and town council about this and they've given their approval—if you decide to do it."

Fletcher drummed his fingers on the table. He was slightly annoyed that Seth had approached him in front of other people, putting him on the spot. He wasn't a certified EMT, but his prior military training and duties had included operating a combat laboratory to treat emergency and trauma patients.

He had always heard and said folks in The Falls always looked out for one another, and now he was being asked to step up and help out. "It's only for one day a week?"

Seth nodded. "One day for eight hours. You'd have to be available for the graveyard shift—ten to six the next morning."

Fletcher stared at Nicole, who met his eyes. Once a week meant sleeping at the barracks behind the police station. "It can't be weekends."

"You can pick any night of the week that fits into your schedule. You'll be directly linked to the 9-1-1 operator."

"Wednesday." It was the first day he'd thought of.

Seth exhaled. "Thanks, buddy. The clerk in the treasurer's office will complete the paperwork and I'll bring it out to the garage for you to sign so they can put you on the payroll."

Nicole's eyebrows lifted when she stared at him across the table.

"What?" Fletcher asked Nicole in a low tone once Seth got up and walked away. "Do you think I'm a glutton for punishment for offering to fill in for the injured EMT?" he asked as she continued to stare at him.

"No, Fletcher," Nicole said after what seemed an interminable pause. "Weren't you the one to remind me that folks in The Falls look out for one another?"

After she'd left The Falls to attend college, each time she returned she saw it in a new light. Nicole thought of it as stuck in time. That if she wanted Starbucks or fast food, she had to get in her car and drive to strip malls off the interstate. When she'd asked her mother if it had been difficult for her to adjust to living in a small town after she'd grown up in Washington, DC, Elizabeth had admitted that because she'd fallen in love and married Andrew Campos, she'd been willing to follow him anywhere.

Nicole had never professed openly that she would never live in Wickham Falls again, because life was just that unpredictable. She could not have imagined her brother succumbing to drug addiction when he'd had a no-tolerance policy with his players. And she'd had no way of knowing she would have to walk away from her position as an associate with one of Miami's leading law firms to become a caregiver for her brother's children.

Fletcher smiled, the dimple in his right cheek deepening with the gesture. “So, you approve?”

She gave him a long, penetrating stare. “Do you really need my approval, Fletcher?”

“I’d like to think I do.”

“Why?”

His smile widened. “Because if we’re going to date, then it’s important we be in agreement when it comes to most situations. Whether you realize it or not, we’re a team.”

Nicole picked up her knife and fork, smiling. “Yay, team!”

Fletcher winked at her. “Hooah!”

She cut into a slice of brisket and put it in her mouth, moaning under her breath as the perfectly smoked meat melted on her tongue. Then she chewed and swallowed a mouthful of potato salad. “The Den should be listed as one of the best barbecue places in the country.”

Fletcher bit into a fall-off-the-bone rib. “That’s what we *don’t* need. Once a place is spotlighted on one of the food channels as the best of, we won’t be able to get in because of a flood of tourists.”

“I didn’t think about that,” she admitted.

Fletcher pointed to her mug. “Do you want another beer?”

She had drunk half of it. “No, thank you.”

Picking up his mug, he drained it and then stood. “I think I’m going to get another beer.”

Nicole stared at his retreating figure as he walked to the bar. With his gorgeous face and magnificent body, she was certain women were not reticent or even shy when attempting to get him to notice them.

She glanced up when a shadow fell across the table. "Hi, Aiden."

Aiden Gibson took the seat Fletcher had vacated. The former navy SEAL removed a black bandanna to reveal cropped blond hair. Aiden had served their country with distinction before returning to The Falls to work alongside his uncle as the Wolf Den's pit master. Tiny lines fanned out around his blue-green eyes when he smiled.

"How long has it been since you graced us with your presence, Captain Campos?"

"Much too long, Chief Petty Officer Gibson."

Aiden's smile faded. "You didn't have to send a note thanking us for donating to Reggie's boys' college fund."

Her brother and Aiden had been teammates on the football team and it had been Aiden who'd set up a GoFundMe page for her nephews' college educations. She'd made it point to mail thank-you cards to everyone who'd donated, no matter how minimal the amount.

"Yes, I did, Aiden. The Camposes and Clarkes are truly overwhelmed by the generosity shown by your family and everyone else in The Falls and Mineral Springs."

"As they say, we folks take care of our own." He covered his head with the bandanna. "I'd better get back to the kitchen before my uncle starts yelling for me." He rose. "Now that you're back, don't be a stranger."

Nicole nodded. "I won't."

Fletcher returned and set a frosty mug on the table. "After we leave here, would you like to come with me to see what I did to Owen Hutchinson's place?"

"I'd love to." She paused. "There's something else I'd like to do."

He angled his head. "What's that?"

"Drive your Blue Flame Special."

Fletcher went completely still as if suddenly impaled by a sharp object. "You want to drive my car?"

Bracing her elbow on the table, Nicole rested her chin on her fist. "Yes. I. Do," she said, stressing each word as if he had a problem understanding her.

He held up both hands at the same time he shook his head. "I can't, Nikki."

"And why not, Fletcher? Are you afraid I'll strip the gears?"

"No, it's not that."

"Then what is it? If I can fly a Blackhawk gunship, I should be able to drive an itty-bitty car."

Fletcher ran a hand across his face. "You're asking the impossible."

She felt a shiver of annoyance wash over her. All she was asking was to drive his car, and he was acting as if she'd asked him for a kidney. "Okay. Forget I asked."

"Gotcha!"

"What!"

"I was teasing you because I needed to know if you would throw a hissy fit if you didn't get your way."

"You weren't teasing me, Fletcher. You were testing me, and I shouldn't have to remind you that I'm a grown-ass woman who doesn't resort to hissy fits or tantrums if she doesn't get what she wants."

Reaching across the table, Fletcher grasped her hand, tightening his grip when she attempted to extricate herself. "Please let me go." They resorted to a stare down until he released her fingers.

Rising slightly, Fletcher reached into a pocket of his jeans and set the keys to the sports car on the table. "The car is yours to keep."

Nicole closed her eyes for several seconds. She didn't know what game he was playing, but it was apparent he wanted to mess with her head. "You're giving me your car?"

He smiled. "Yes. Consider it a peace offering."

"I don't need another car. Besides, it would never suit my lifestyle. Where would Othello sit?"

Fletcher slapped his forehead with the heel of his hand. "I forgot about your four-legged boyfriend."

"Othello's not my boyfriend, but my protector. Only you can be my boyfriend."

A beat passed. "What if I want to be your boyfriend and your protector? But only if you will permit me to be."

"Do you really believe I need protecting?" Nicole questioned.

"Every woman, no matter how solvent or independent she may be or feel, needs a man to protect her."

Her eyebrows lifted. "You sound like a throwback to another generation."

Fletcher smiled. "I know, but I'm okay with it. Are you okay with me wanting to play superhero?"

Nicole placed her hand over his fisted one. "Yes, but only if you don't let anyone see your cape."

He reversed their hands, brought hers to his mouth and dropped a kiss on the knuckles. "You're the only one who will get to see it."

They shared a smile and then concentrated on the food on their plates. Nicole did not want to fight with Fletcher, but she also didn't want him to think she was a helpless damsel in distress waiting around for him to rescue her from the bad guys.

"Do you want seconds?"

Nicole patted her belly at the same time she shook her head. "Please, no. I'm as full as a tick."

"Careful, sweetheart. Your country is showing," Fletcher teased.

She ignored the endearment when she said, "I've never pretended to be anything other than country. The instant I open my mouth to speak, folks know I'm from the South."

"I happen to like country girls."

"And I happen to like country boys masquerading as superheroes."

"Am I Batman, Captain America, Superman or Black Panther?"

"Aquaman."

"Why him?"

"You and Jason Momoa both have multiple tattoos."

"So, you like ink?" Fletcher teased.

Nicole extended her right hand to show him the USMC tattoo stamped on the underside. "I do, but after I got this one, I couldn't decide at the time whether I wanted to get another tattoo."

"If you were to get more ink now, what would it be?"

"I'd put the scales of justice on my left wrist."

"I still say you should've been JAG."

Nicole stared at the tattoo on her wrist. "That would've meant not resigning my commission."

"Do you ever regret leaving the corps?"

Fletcher was asking Nicole the very question she'd asked herself once she'd submitted her separation papers, and the answer was the same. She had mulled over leaving for a very long time and, in the end, had known she had made the right decision.

"No." Her answer appeared to satisfy Fletcher's curiosity when he picked up his mug, gave her a mock salute and took a long swallow.

She wanted to tell him she'd never been impulsive when it came to anything that would affect her future. The exception was leaving the law firm to come to Wickham Falls to take care of her brother and nephews.

The restaurant was becoming more and more crowded when she suggested they give up their booth to newcomers. She picked up the keys to the Corvette and walked out of the restaurant to the parking lot while Fletcher stayed behind to pay the bill.

Chapter Seven

Fletcher stared out the windshield at the passing landscape as Nicole accelerated along a winding two-lane road in an area favored by hunters. She handled the powerful sports car like an expert driver and there was no doubt her reflexes hadn't slowed since becoming a civilian. The skills she'd acquired as a gunship helicopter pilot were on full display as she navigated a sharp hillside curve that had him unconsciously braking when she hadn't.

"Nicely done, speed racer."

"Thank you," she said, not taking her eyes off the road.

"It looks as if I'm not the only adrenaline junkie."

"I never said I wasn't one," Nicole admitted.

When he'd left the Wolf Den, Nicole had taken off her cap and was seated in the Corvette waiting for him.

Instead of reversing direction, she'd driven through Mineral Springs and headed for the forested area locals and tourists used for hunting and fishing.

Fletcher did not complain because it would increase the time they would spend together. The one thing he'd noticed about the adult Nicole was that she was confident enough to say whatever was on her mind. She hadn't been reticent when she'd said she did not need him to protect her. And she was right because he'd never protected her—not even when he'd overheard girls talking about her being stuck-up.

It had taken nearly two decades for him to come to know Nicole. Unlike many families in Johnson County, the Camposes did not claim generations of coal miners, but professionals who'd gone into education and law. He'd told her kids were afraid of her father exacting tough justice, but the truth was she'd been alienated because they were jealous of her intelligence and envious that boys whispered about how cute she was.

"If you were to sell this car, how much would it go for?" Nicole asked, breaking into his thoughts.

"About sixty thousand."

Nicole smiled as she eased off the gas pedal. "Not bad for a car that's more than sixty years old. If you don't mind my asking, what is the most expensive car you've restored and sold?"

Fletcher thought about her question for a moment. "My representative sold one for one thirty-five."

She gave him a quick glance before focusing on the road again. "You have an agent?"

"He searches out cars for me, I restore them, and he gets his commission once they're sold. Most times he puts them up for auction, which generates higher profits for both of us."

"On average, how much have you invested in restoring a vehicle?"

"It can be as low as a couple of thousand to more than ten."

"That's not too shabby if you're able to recoup your outlay appreciably."

"Pop calls it my side hustle, but I tell him don't hate it, because I'm saving the money for my retirement."

Fletcher mentioning retirement reminded Nicole that Austen Auto & Sons had been a family-owned business for more than a century when his great-great-grandfather had set up shop to repair one of the first Model T Fords in Wickham Falls. The business had been passed down from father to son and then grandson, and now there was just Fletcher and his father.

Reggie kept her up-to-date about the residents of their hometown, and she'd been surprised when he'd told her that Sean Austen had moved his family to Texas to work on an oil rig. She knew Fletcher had many more years before he would consider retiring and wondered if he didn't marry or father a son, whether he would sell the shop or go out of business.

"You have quite a few years before you even consider retiring."

"I'm projecting by sixty-five I should be more than ready to hang up my tools. Pop just turned sixty and he claims he's going to hang in for another three or four years, then he's done. What about you, Nikki?" Fletcher asked. "Have you thought about what you want to do once you retire?"

"Not really. It would depend on my marital status."

"You want to get married?"

Nicole thought she imagined a hint of surprise in his voice. "I never said I didn't want to be married."

"I…I just thought that…" His words trailed off.

"You thought what, Fletcher?" Nicole asked as she slowed the car to just under the legal speed limit.

"That you weren't willing to give up a career for marriage."

"Why can't I have both? My grandmother was a teacher and my mother clerked for a judge, and both had husbands and children. So why should it be any different with me?"

"I suppose it wouldn't be any different with you."

"You suppose? Either you believe I can or I can't."

"You are a pilot and a lawyer, so there's probably nothing you can't do."

Nicole blew him an air kiss. "You're really good for a woman's ego."

Fletcher rested his left arm over the back of her seat. "I don't want to be good for your ego, but good to you, Nikki. I want us to have as much fun as we can before you leave to go back to Florida."

"On a scale of one to ten, how much fun are you talking about?"

Fletcher ran his fingers up and down her nape and Nicole clamped her teeth together to smother a moan. He unknowingly had discovered one of her erogenous zones.

"How about a fifteen?"

"I kind of like the sound of that. Can you give me a hint what you plan for us?"

"Nah."

"Why not, Fletcher?"

"Because I want to surprise you."

Nicole wanted to tell Fletcher she did not like surprises, but she was curious about what he had planned for them to do during her stay. "O-kay," she said, drawing out the two syllables. "I suppose I'll just have to wait and see."

Leaning to his left, Fletcher kissed her cheek. "Yes, you will."

"You claim you can cook a little." He nodded. "I want to know if you're going to cook for me."

"Keep fishing, Nikki, but I'm not biting."

"You can't blame me for trying."

He released her neck. "Yeah, right, Counselor. And I'm not going to let you wear me down."

"Let me warn you that I can be pretty persuasive."

"What do you have planned?" Fletcher asked.

Nicole shook her head. "Nah. If I told you, then it wouldn't be a surprise."

She felt as if she and Fletcher had turned back the clock to when they were in high school before he'd asked her to prom. They'd worked well together. He'd respected her suggestions and decisions and she his, but at no time had he indicated he'd liked her as more than a classmate. His asking her to prom had come as a complete shock.

"I've also planned several outings with Luke and Danny. Of course, you're included."

Nicole smiled sweetly. "Thank you so much."

Her nephews had spent the past two weekends with their grandparents, and although they enjoyed playing with their cousins, both had complained about not going anywhere, although she had given their grandfather money to offset the cost of taking them out to eat or to the movies. They had gotten used to her taking them out on weekends. Whether to eat at Ruthie's, to go to a movie, or just on a road trip to stop at roadside stands to buy fruits and vegetables, or to go berry picking.

Nicole gasped when she pulled up in front of what had been the Hutchinson property. A two-story farmhouse with a wraparound porch had replaced the small run-down structure that had been no larger than a bungalow. Rays from the late-summer afternoon sun bathed the white vinyl siding in gold. Navy blue trim matched the window shutters.

"What do you think?" Fletcher asked.

"It's incredible," she said softly. A colorful floral wreath adorned the front door and a quartet of white rockers with cushioned seats and backrests in monochromatic shades of blue beckoned one to come and sit awhile.

"Let's go in."

Nicole shut off the engine, handed Fletcher the keys and exited the Corvette, before following him up the steps to the porch. She gasped again when he unlocked and opened the door to an open floorplan with gleaming cherrywood flooring. She had expected to find Fletcher's home to be the quintessential bachelor residence with sofas and chairs covered in dark-hued leather, not gaily colored and patterned fabrics.

Kicking off her running shoes, she walked across the living room and into the all-white kitchen with its stainless-steel Viking appliances and gray quartz countertops and backsplashes. The gray stone floor tiles were cool under her bare feet. Nicole ran her fingers over the smooth countertop on the breakfast bar overlooking the cooking island.

"You must love cooking here."

Fletcher came over to stand next to her. "I do. I'm still learning, but I'm having fun trying new dishes. You'll have to let me know what you want and I'll try to whip it up for you."

Nicole gave him a sidelong glance. "How much advance notice do I have to give you?"

He lifted broad shoulders under the black T-shirt. "Only a couple of days. What would you like me to make for you?"

"Fajitas. I love Mexican food and fajitas are one of my favorite dishes."

Fletcher moved closer until their shoulders were touching. "Steak, chicken or shrimp?"

Tilting her chin, she smiled up at him. "It doesn't matter."

"Will the boys eat fajitas or should I make something different for them?"

A small laugh escaped Nicole's parted lips. "They will definitely eat fajitas."

"That's good to know."

Fletcher stared at her from under lowered lids at the same time he angled his head until their lips were mere inches apart. He was so close that Nicole could inhale his breath. She knew he was going to kiss her and she wanted him to. She wasn't certain why he'd selected her as his temporary romantic interest, but at that moment she did not care.

Her girlhood crush on Fletcher came back like the rushing waters of the falls that had given their town its name. She stared at his firm lips and then closed her eyes when his mouth covered hers in a caress that ignited a wave of heat that surged through her body like a lit fuse. Time and reason stopped when she found herself in his embrace, mouths joined as he lifted her off her feet and deepened the kiss. Her arms went around his neck and she held on to Fletcher as if he were her lifeline. All her senses were heightened when she inhaled the lingering scent of his masculine cologne on his warm skin.

The kiss ended and Nicole pressed her cheek to his, feeling the stubble against her smooth one. "Why did you kiss me?"

"I'm surprised you have to ask me that," Fletcher said. He set her on her feet but did not release her. "I've waited more than seventeen years to kiss you."

She blinked once and then closed her eyes against his direct stare. The amber orbs had darkened until they reminded her of tiny cups of espresso. "If I'd gone to prom with you, then you probably wouldn't have had to wait this long."

Fletcher smiled. "You're right about that."

Nicole rested her forehead against his chest. "I'd like to see the rest of your house."

She knew it wasn't safe—at least for her—to remain in his embrace for much longer. Being this close to Fletcher was a blatant reminder of how long it had been since a man had kissed her. Fletcher's kiss wasn't as much about passion as it was to gauge her reaction. It was also a test for her. Because she'd kissed him back.

Fletcher released her waist and laced her fingers through his. "We'll start upstairs and work our way down."

Nicole walked with him as he led her up the staircase

covered in a plush delft-blue pile. The carpeting continued down the hallway along the second story. "Who decorated your home?"

"I hired a professional. I told her I wanted furnishings I could live with year after year. I thought I was being interviewed for a position with a company when she gave me a questionnaire about my likes and dislikes. Once I completed it, she said it was a personality and lifestyle profile."

Nicole enjoyed the feel of the carpet pile between her toes. "What did it conclude?"

"That I'm a traditionalist and basically a homebody. I like entertaining, but don't want lots of folks traipsing through my home, so she suggested an outdoor kitchen and bathroom."

"Do you have a cleaning service? Because this place is spotless."

Fletcher gave her fingers a gentle squeeze. "No."

"You clean it?"

"Yes. I like cleanliness and everything in its place. My mother taught me to cook and the army to clean. For me, that's a win-win."

"What's going to happen when you have kids, Fletcher? Are you going to go behind them with a broom and dustpan sweeping up crumbs?"

He chuckled. "No. I'm not that bad. I believe in letting kids be kids. They can run and scream and generally make a mess."

"Are you saying you're going to be an indulgent father?"

Fletcher stopped on the landing and met Nicole's eyes. "The only thing I'm going to say is that I hope and pray I'll become a positive role model, but I will definitely need help from their mother."

Nicole felt as if he was trying to draw a response from her. Interacting with the mature Fletcher Austen made her aware that he was a very complex man; that he wasn't easy to know. She had found him direct and forthcoming, yet it was what he didn't say that had her attempting to analyze a part of him that he kept hidden from her.

She knew he'd liked her enough to ask her to prom, and over the years, she'd asked herself why, when he could have taken any girl in their school who wasn't coupled up with another boy. "You're a good catch, Fletcher, and I'm sure you'll find that special woman who will become your wife and the mother of your children."

A hint of a smile tilted the corners of his mouth. "Thanks for the vote of confidence."

Nicole also smiled. "There's no need to thank me. You've got what it takes, so just own it." She wondered how her life, their lives, would have changed if she had accepted Fletcher's invitation to be his prom date. Would they have kept in touch with each other during their time in the military? Would he have become her first lover? Would she, eventually, have become his wife and the mother of their children?

She shook her head as if to rid her thoughts of anything that resembled permanence with Fletcher. She had agreed to date him and had not ruled out sleeping with him, but that was where it would end. Nicole was determined not to let her heart overrule her head as it had in the past when she'd fallen in love with a man she could not have because he'd belonged to another woman.

"How many bedrooms do you have?" Nicole asked Fletcher as he led her down the hallway.

"Three. The master and two guest bedrooms."

Enough for a couple and their two or three children, she thought. It was obvious Fletcher had planned for his future, while hers was in limbo. She did not regret having to step in and become temporary guardian for her nephews because not only had they lost their mother, but their father was also in crisis. She had reminded Reggie that she would remain in Wickham Falls for as long as it took for him to get clean, so there was no need to concern himself about the well-being of his sons. After all, she did not have a job waiting for her, she was able to pay the maintenance on her condo online and her mother had made it a practice to check on her town home at least once a week.

Nicole walked into Fletcher's bedroom and went completely still. Pale blue-gray walls provided the backdrop for a king-size bed with a quilted headboard in a smoky gray. Muted hues of white, blue and gray dominated window shutters, bed dressings, the geometric patterns on the armchairs and the padded bench seat at the foot of the bed. Solid-colored throw pillows accentuated the furnishings. The expansive suite also included a bathroom with a double vanity, garden tub with Jacuzzi, shower stall and a private alcove for the commode and bidet. The skylight over the tub area provided a canopy of light for the entire space.

The two smaller bedrooms were just as impressive. One with a full-size and single bed, and the other with twin beds; both claimed en suite baths. Furnishings in monochromatic shades of pinks and blues identified spaces for his nieces and nephews. She'd noticed that all the rooms had window shutters, gas fireplaces, ceiling fans and walk-in closets, while the guest rooms had area rugs, love seats and armchairs.

She was equally impressed with the living, dining and family rooms on the first floor. The door from the garage led into a mud/laundry room with a connecting fully stocked pantry. Fletcher had set up an alcove outside the kitchen as a home/office/library. She noted many of the subjects of the books lining built-in shelves included business, finance, accounting and automobiles. The talented decorator had created the perfect template for sophisticated, casual family living.

Nicole smothered a gasp of surprise when she walked into the outdoor kitchen with its six-burner grill, wood-burning pizza oven, sink, refrigerator, barbecue pit, smoker and firepit. The outdoor dining table with six driftwood wicker chairs, along with a matching love seat, chaise, ottoman and coffee table sat on an indoor/outdoor rug stamped with pine leaves was conducive to outdoor relaxing and entertaining. A collection of glass hurricane lanterns lined the wall enclosing the patio, while ferns and succulents overflowed from terra-cotta planters. She opened the door in a corner of the patio to discover the bathroom with a vanity sink and commode.

Nicole folded her body down to the Haitian cotton cushion on the chaise, wiggling her bare toes. The patio was the ideal place to begin or end the day. “I could hang out here for hours.”

Fletcher sat next to her, reached over and eased her legs across his thigh. “You can come and hang out here whenever you want,” he said, repeating what she’d similarly told him about coming to her home to eat.

"I hope when you bring your nephews over that y'all will plan to spend the night."

She sat straight. "Is that what you want?"

He nodded. "It's what I'd like. Once we begin to play board games, it may go on for hours."

"Which games are you talking about?"

"When I asked Luke and Danny which board games, they said Monopoly, Uno and Sequence."

"That's because we usually play games after dinner on Sundays."

Fletcher massaged her instep, sending shivers up and down her spine. "I have Monopoly and Uno, but not Sequence. I went online and ordered Sequence, dominoes and a checkers and chess board. My siblings and I were very competitive when it came to board games. We'd chart our wins and losses on a chalkboard. My brother was the chess champ and my sister was right behind him in checkers. I became the all-around Monopoly champion because I'd memorized the board and knew how much money they had to buy properties."

"Isn't that the same as counting cards? Which, by the way, is a no-go at casinos."

Fletcher angled his head. "It wasn't about how I won, but that I'd won."

Nicole's jaw dropped. "No, you didn't say that."

"I didn't cheat, Nikki. I just used whatever skills I had to win. Do you remember Louis Brown?"

She nodded. "He was our valedictorian."

"Louis tried to hide it, but he had an eidetic memory. He could recall everything he saw or read. He'd become a walking encyclopedia and, after a while, the teachers stopped calling on him because he knew all the answers. I don't have an eidetic memory, but if I see the same thing over and over, I'm able to remember it."

Nicole narrowed her eyes. "I hope you don't scam my nephews when playing Monopoly."

"How do you know they won't scam me?" Fletcher countered.

"My nephews are not scammers!" she said in defense of the boys.

Fletcher tightened his hold on her feet as she went completely still. "Whoa! Easy, Mama Bear. I meant no harm. I'm sorry."

The stiffness went out of her body and it was a full minute before Nicole could bring herself to accept Fletcher's apology. "I forgive you."

Fletcher realized he had made a serious faux pas. He was forced to remember their special circumstances. And he had to continually remind himself of their tragedies. Leaning over, he pressed a kiss to her cheek. "I am really sorry, Nikki. I'm going inside to brew some coffee. Would you like to have some?"

"Yes, please."

"Do you want to come inside or drink it out here?"

Nicole's expression softened, the lashes that had shadowed her high cheekbones flying up. Rays from the sun fell over her delicate face, causing Fletcher's breath to catch in his lungs. At that moment there was something about her that appeared almost angelic. Her large dark eyes, round face, pert nose and lushly curved mouth reminded him of several of his sister's favorite dolls.

Fletcher had told himself that he liked Nicole Campos, but that was only a half-truth. Yes, he did like her but the more time he spent with her, the more he realized he was falling in love with her. Everything about Nicole appealed to him: her natural beauty, intelligence, confidence and her unwavering loyalty to those she loved. He'd wanted to ask her about the men in her life, yet hadn't wanted to bring up something that would put a wall between them.

He released her feet and stood. "Regular or decaf?"

"Regular, please."

"Is milk and sugar okay?"

Nicole's head popped up and she smiled. "Both."

Fletcher nodded. "I'll be back." He returned to the house and walked into the kitchen. The day had been filled with pleasant surprises. He knew he had shocked a few guys at the Den when he'd entered with Nicole, because it was the first time since he'd returned to The Falls as a civilian that he had come to the restaurant with a woman. When Dwight Adams had mentioned he was keeping Nicole company to stave off guys attempting to hit on his girlfriend, Fletcher had no intention of denying she was his girlfriend.

Despite agreeing to go out with him, Fletcher wondered if Nicole would be willing to take their friendship to another level. The question wasn't "Would she?" It was more "Would *he* be content to share a bed with Nicole and then remain unaffected when it came time for her to leave?"

He washed his hands and filled the coffee grinder with beans as he contemplated whether it would be best if they had a strictly platonic relationship. He knew he was overthinking something that would never materialize and decided to let things unfold naturally. Every other weekend he would get together with Nicole and her nephews and on the off weekends it would be just the two of them.

He brewed two cups of coffee, added turbinado sugar and foamed milk, and carried them to the patio. He handed one to Nicole. “One café au lait for the lady.”

Smiling, she held it with both hands. “Oh, I think I’m going to keep you around for a while. It smells delicious.”

Fletcher sat close to Nicole and stretched out his legs. “I’m not quite a barista, but after I bought the espresso machine, I experimented making lattes and cappuccinos.”

Nicole touched her cup to his before putting it to her mouth. “How did they come out?” she asked after taking a sip.

He lifted broad shoulders. “Okay.”

“Just okay?”

Fletcher took a sip from his cup. “The only thing I’m going to say is that I’m a work in progress. I’m much better at making s’mores using the firepit.”

Nicole’s eyes lit up like a child’s on Christmas morning when seeing gaily wrapped presents under the tree. “Did you say s’mores?”

“Yes, I did. Why?”

“They are my favorite dessert snack.”

“I don’t have all the ingredients on hand, but the next time you come, I’ll definitely make them for you.”

She held out her little finger. “Pinky swear?”

Fletcher ignored her finger, slanted his head and kissed her parted lips. “Yes.”

Nicole lowered her eyes and ran the tip of her tongue over her lips, bringing his gaze to linger there. Shifting slightly, he managed to put a modicum of space between them as he sipped his coffee.

The smell of freshly mowed grass lingered in the air. He had gotten up at dawn to cut the grass before it got too hot. His house sat on a quarter of an acre and, after he'd erected a fence, Fletcher was afforded complete privacy from his nearest neighbors.

"How often do you sit out here?" Nicole asked.

"Not often enough," Fletcher admitted. "I come home and make dinner for myself then veg out in front the television to catch up on the news and sporting events."

"When do you work on your cars?"

He turned to stare at her. "I leave that for the weekends."

"And now we're intruding on your weekends."

"Do you hear me complaining, Nikki? I don't have a timetable when I have to complete restoring the Studebaker because my rep hasn't found a buyer. Once he calls and tells me someone wants it, I'll devote a lot more time to getting it ready. Is there anything else you'd like to know about me?" Fletcher asked when she stared straight ahead.

"Yes," Nicole said after a pregnant pause.

"What is it?"

"Why me, Fletcher? Why are you hanging out with me when there a lot of other women in Wickham Falls you could be with?"

He set his half-empty cup on the coffee table and gave her an incredulous stare. "You wait until now to ask me that?"

"Yes."

Fletcher shook his head as he crossed his arms over his chest. "Did it ever dawn on you that if I'd wanted to be with another woman, it would've happened before you returned to Wickham Falls?"

"Yes, but—"

"But nothing, Nicole," he snapped, cutting her off. "Do you always attempt to sabotage your relationships even before they begin?"

She pressed her lips together in what he interpreted as anger. "Who said anything about a relationship?"

Fletcher was annoyed with Nicole. It was as if she'd turned the clock back more than seventeen years. "Should I have used *liaison* instead of *relationship*?"

Nicole stared at him, unblinking. "*Liaison* is better than *relationship*."

He wanted to remind Nicole that Dwight had already referred to her as his girlfriend and she hadn't seemed bothered by it. "Just what is it you're afraid of, Nikki?" His voice was low and soothing. "What happened between you and the man you loved and lost?"

"I never had him."

Fletcher moved closer, took the cup from her hand and set it beside his on the coffee table. He effortlessly shifted her to sit across his lap. "Tell me about it, sweetheart."

Chapter Eight

Nicole opened her mouth but no sound came out. It was as if her throat had constricted, because shame and embarrassment had temporarily rendered her mute. "I got involved with a married man and it almost cost me my commission."

She told Fletcher about the lifer master sergeant who'd sought her out to talk about the anxiety he was experiencing following a number of deployments. She had urged him to talk to the base's psychiatrist, but he was afraid they would deem him unfit for service and recommend a medical discharge.

"How many years did he have in?" Fletcher asked.

"Twenty-one. He was trying for thirty, but I knew he would never make it because he was experiencing PTSD. He had a wife, six kids and several grandchildren living together and depending on his allotments."

Fletcher tightened his hold around Nicole's body. "That's a lot of responsibility for one man to shoulder."

She nodded. "That was the root cause of his anxiety. He had become their personal ATM and every time he got an email from them it was always about money. I'd become his shoulder to cry on and, before I knew it, we had bonded emotionally."

"Were you in love with him, Nikki?"

She nodded. "I loved him, but I wasn't in love with him. One morning my commanding officer summoned me to his office and read me the riot act about fraternizing with an enlistee. He said if it did not stop, I would face court-martial. That's when I knew I had to cut him off cold."

"What happened after that?"

"He'd signed up for his fifth deployment and was killed when he stepped on an IED. There was a lot of controversy surrounding his death because the incendiary explosive device had been uncovered and they were waiting for the bomb squad to disarm it."

"Are you saying he committed suicide so his family would get his death benefit?"

Easing back, Nicole met Fletcher's eyes. "I know he did. I got a letter from him after he'd been shipped out that said in so many words that he loved me and that he was also was going to solve his family's financial problems. I burned the letter because I didn't want anyone to find it and jeopardize his family getting his death allowance. He was given a military funeral with full honors befitting a hero and buried at Arlington National Cemetery. His passing bothered me for a long time because I thought I hadn't done enough to help him."

Nicole had continued to second-guess herself on the

anniversary of his death when she should've reported him either to the chaplain or the psychiatrist for counseling. The pressure of providing financial support and becoming an enabler for his adult children, who'd refused to seek gainful employment, had overwhelmed him. He'd believed suicide was his only way to remedy the situation.

Fletcher dropped a kiss on her hair. "You can't beat yourself up about something over which you had no control."

"I know that now." Nicole didn't want to admit to Fletcher that the incident had impacted her subsequent relationships with men. She refused to listen to them complain about ex-wives or girlfriends, demanding bosses or clashes with their children. She didn't dump on them about her problems and she had made it known she did not want to hear about theirs.

"How well did you get along with Othello's handler?"

Nicole smiled, grateful that she no longer had to talk about her involvement with a man she'd loved for the wrong reason. "Keith and I were in NROTC together. We managed to keep in touch even after graduation. He applied to SEAL school and made it. His birthday is coming up mid-October and I've committed to drive to Kentucky to help him celebrate. I plan to take the boys and Othello with me."

"Othello will probably be happy to see him again."

"It will be the first time they see each other since I adopted him, and there's no doubt it will be a wonderful reunion for both." Nicole paused and then said, "If you're not busy, would you like to come with us? His sister says he spends a lot of time alone and I think he would appreciate talking to someone who can relate to what he's been through."

"You have to let me know when and how long you plan to stay."

"Rachel has made plans for us to stay overnight. If you do decide to come, you'll have to pack your jammies."

A slight frown appeared between Fletcher eyes. "I don't own a pair of pajamas."

"No jammies, no can come," she teased. "You and the boys will share a bedroom and they don't need to see your naked hind parts."

"That wouldn't be good. I suppose I'll have to buy a pair or two. What about you, Nikki? Do you ever sleep in your birthday suit?"

She scrunched up her nose. "Hardly ever now that I'm living with Daniel and Luke."

"What about when you're home in Miami?"

Nicole sobered quickly. "What are you implying, Fletcher? Do you want to know if I'm sleeping with someone?"

"Wow! You're really direct, aren't you?"

"Would you like me if I wasn't?"

He smiled. "No. I like the fact you say exactly what's on your mind."

"I'm not seeing anyone right now, because I don't need a man monitoring my whereabouts or one whose aim is to dominate me when I'm quite comfortable being a single woman with options as to what I want to do with my life. I can choose to live anywhere, and there are a number of states where I can practice law because I've taken and passed the multiple-state bar exam."

"Would you ever consider moving back to The Falls if you decided to leave Miami?"

"I haven't ruled anything out," Nicole said. "If Reggie needs me to stay after he comes back, then I will. I like working for Preston McAvoy, which means I'm still a practicing attorney." She didn't see the beginnings of a smile tip the corners of Fletcher's mouth when he lowered his head.

Nicole had been forthcoming when she'd admitted to him that she had never been in love or even close to it. There were times she'd believed she was incapable of the sentiment. She was totally vested in duty and honor, which had forced her to remain detached from emotions that would compromise the operation to which she had been assigned. She had learned to give and take orders and to follow them without question.

There were officers who'd expressed an interest in her, but Nicole had not wanted to get involved with someone in her unit. She was content to socialize with them in the officers' club, but drew the line when it came to a physical relationship.

Whenever she'd returned home during an official leave, she reunited with one of her former college classmates in Washington, DC. Morgan Jackson.

They'd been friends with benefits until shortly before her first deployment and, for Nicole, it was enough. Morgan was the closest Nicole had gotten to forming a stable relationship with a man.

"Don't you ever let a man tell you that you're not a remarkable woman, Nikki."

She rested a hand on Fletcher's jaw, feeling the emerging stubble against her palm. "As I said before, you're wonderful for a woman's ego. You're going to have to let me go because I need to get home and feed Othello."

Fletcher gathered Nicole in his arms, stood and held her until her bare feet touched the rug. "One of these days you should bring him over so he can have the run of the backyard."

Nicole smiled up at him. "Whenever I let him out, his favorite pastime is chasing squirrels."

"Does he kill them?"

"No."

"Well, instead of chasing squirrels he'll have a family of rabbits to intimidate. Once I had the landscapers clear the backyard, I discovered several brown rabbits coming out of a hole. I counted three, but now there are a lot more."

Nicole picked up the coffee cups and headed for the house. "What's the expression? Multiply like rabbits."

Fletcher followed Nicole and reached over her head to open the sliding door leading directly into the kitchen. "If they become too numerous, I'll have to set traps and take them to a guy in Mineral Springs who raises rabbits for restaurants."

"Rabbit, squirrel, possum are definitely not a part of my diet," Nicole said over her shoulder.

He watched her slip into her running shoes and then scoop up her wristlet off the countertop. "What about venison, rattlesnake or alligator?"

"Venison, yes, but no to the alligator and snake."

"Where's your sense of adventure, sweetheart?"

"I have more than my share of adventure piloting helicopters in Afghanistan while attempting to avoid being shot down by RPGs."

Fletcher did not want to believe he'd been so callous when mentioning her disdain for adventure. Each and every time Nicole had taken off in a helicopter, she had become a target for rocket-propelled grenades. She had begun her career as a pilot medic evacuating the wounded to field hospitals before being promoted to piloting helicopter gunships. And if one of her suitors had sought to tame her, then he'd either been a complete idiot or his ego had surpassed whatever common sense he'd believed he had.

He also wondered how many men had underestimated Nicole's ability to not only take care of herself but also others. He had talked about protecting her when he should've said caring for her. After all, there was a difference. Reaching for the house and car keys, Fletcher led her out to the car.

The drive to her house was accomplished in complete silence, and Fletcher wondered what Nicole was thinking. He'd spent most of the afternoon and early evening with her.

"What are you smiling about?"

Fletcher glanced over at Nicole. He hadn't realized he was smiling. "I was thinking about kissing you."

"Should I assume you enjoyed it?"

"It was most excellent," he said, his smile becoming a wide grin.

Nicole turned to stare out the side window. "I liked it, too."

"Hot damn!" he whispered.

She turned back to him. "You're going to have to watch your language when you're around the boys, because every once in a while, they let something slip out they shouldn't be saying."

"What do you do about it?"

"There are times when I ignore it, but if it gets to be too much then it's a long-winded lecture. And if they continue, I ground them, which seems to do the trick until the next time."

"The first time I cursed in front my father he warned me that if I was man enough to use that language then I was man enough to move out of his house and take care of myself."

"How old were you?"

"Either nine or ten. It wasn't what he said but how he'd it said that scared me. I really thought he was going to put me out."

"I suppose it worked."

"Damn straight it did. It was only years later when I asked if he was serious, he admitted that my mother would've divorced him if he'd followed through with his threat. That's when I knew my mother, and not Pop, was the boss of the house."

"It was the same in my house," Nicole admitted. "Whenever I'd ask my father if I could do something, he would say to ask my mother or 'What did your mom say?'"

Fletcher turned off onto the road leading to Nicole's house, not wanting his time with her to end. She wasn't scheduled to pick up her nephews until the following afternoon, and that meant he could've invited her to spend the night with him. Of course, he would have offered her one of the bedrooms, but he wanted to experience what it would feel like to wake up and find her under his roof.

She had asked him why her and not some other woman. Although he had accused her of attempting to sabotage their relationship even before it could begin, he'd wanted to ask why not her. Did she believe she wasn't worthy of a man's love? That she could go through her life without experiencing what it meant to love and be loved?

Fletcher had had his share of false starts when he'd believed he was falling in love with a woman and tried to convince himself that she was the one when she wasn't. And not once had he ever confused passion for love. After a while he'd come to realize he was trying much too hard to find that special woman with whom to share his life and future.

Perhaps it had been the uncertainty whether he would live to serve thirty years before separating from the military that had made him anxious about marrying and starting a family. It was only after his injury that he'd had time to reflect on his contribution to his family, friends and his country. Fletcher had returned to Wickham Falls to pick up the mantle of operating Austen Auto & Sons. He had also proved that he'd planned to put down roots once he'd purchased property.

He maneuvered into the driveway and cut off the engine. Fletcher was out of the car and had come around to assist Nicole before she'd unsnapped her seat belt. He walked with her up the porch and to the door. She'd just opened the door when Othello came out to greet her. Whining, the dog sniffed her legs before he repeated the action with Fletcher.

Reaching down, he scratched the canine behind the ears. "Hey, buddy." Othello rose on his hind legs and Fletcher rubbed his back. Under the fur was powerful muscle. Nicole's expression registered shock as he continued to bond with her pet.

"I've never known him to take to someone so quickly."

Fletcher smiled at her. "He must know that we were both military warriors."

Nicole kicked off her shoes. "Do you want to come in and feed him before you take him for a walk?"

"Of course. We dudes have to stick together."

Her eyebrow quirked slightly. "So now you are besties?"

"You bet. One of these days I'm going to bring him over to my place where he can run and chase rabbits."

Bending, Fletcher took off his boots and left them on the mat next to Nicole's running shoes. He waited with Othello outside the kitchen while she opened a can of dog food and a bag of dry kibbles and placed them in a dish alongside a bowl of fresh water on a rubber mat.

Fletcher sat on the floor, his back braced against the wall as he watched the Belgian Malinois finish off the food before drinking most of the water. Othello came over to him, sat and rested his muzzle on Fletcher's thigh. It was the action Nicole said would signify the dog's complete acceptance of him.

He ran his hand over the thick fur covering the dog's back. "You and I are going to have a good time together. I'm going to have to ask your mama when you can come and hang out with Uncle Fletcher."

Nicole, sitting on a stool at the breakfast bar, glared at him. "You will not take my dog."

"I don't want to take him. We just want to do a little male bonding. Right, boy," Fletcher crooned as he continued to stroke Othello. The dog stood and walked to the front door.

Nicole slipped off the stool. "It's time for his walk. Wait here and I'll get his leash and poop bag."

Fletcher let Othello take the lead during their leisurely walk. It gave him the opportunity to survey the neighborhood where Nicole and her brother had grown up. Most of the homes were designed with two or three stories and front porches.

Signs advertising security companies were visible on most lawns, while a number of cameras were also evident. Rural, small-town Wickham Falls was not exempt from the explosion of substance abuse, and residents took steps to protect their lives and property. There had been a time when people did not lock their cars or their front doors, but that was in the past.

Even though events in his hometown had changed, Fletcher discovered most of the residents hadn't. Their concern was earning enough money to support their families and keeping a close eye on their children to make certain they didn't fall prey to drugs and completed high school.

Othello saw a squirrel and took off like a shot, Fletcher racing to keep up with him. The furry rodent scurried up a tree while Othello excitedly barked. "It's all right, buddy. He's gone."

Fortunately, Fletcher's leg hadn't buckled with the unexpected sprint. He religiously performed the recommended exercise prescribed by his orthopedist to strengthen the muscles in his injured leg. However, occasionally he overdid it and had to sit in the Jacuzzi to ease the discomfort.

He and Othello returned to the house and found Nicole sitting on the porch. She'd left a bowl of cold water on the floor for the dog. "How was your walk?"

Fletcher sat on the rocker opposite her. "Good until Othello decided to chase a squirrel."

Nicole tented her fingers. "I should've warned you that he can take off without warning when he sees one."

"Can he be trained not to chase them?"

"If you command him to stay, he'll stop."

Fletcher knew military dogs were trained to obey one handler and, once discharged, had to be retrained to adapt to life as a civilian. Resting his head against the back of the rocker, he closed his eyes. A wave of calmness swept over him as he drew in a deep breath. It was as if all his senses were heightened when he heard the slip-slap of tires on the roadway from a passing car, the tweeting of birds in the nearby tree and the faint chirping of crickets.

"Don't expect me to lift you if you fall asleep."

Fletcher opened his eyes and smiled at her. "I was just resting my eyes."

She returned his smile. "That's what the boys say when they fall asleep while watching television."

He pushed to his feet. "I think it's time I head home." Walking to Nicole, he leaned over and kissed her cheek. "Thanks for making today special."

Nicole looked up at him through her lashes. "Same here. What time do you want me to bring the boys over Saturday?"

"I'm always up early, so it can be any time you want. Don't forget to bring Othello."

She narrowed one eye. "Are you trying to lure my pet away from me?"

Fletcher held up both hands. "No!"

"I don't believe you, Fletcher."

He wanted to tell Nicole he would never accept ownership of Othello unless she was a part of the deal. "Believe me, babe."

Turning on his heel, Fletcher walked off the porch, got into the Corvette and drove away.

He had been truthful when he'd told Nicole that she had made the day special.

She had answered a lot of questions for him when she'd told him about the man with whom she had become emotionally involved. And Fletcher wondered what it was in the older man that had made her risk her career. Was it naivete, compassion or genuine concern?

He returned home, parked the Corvette in the garage and disarmed the system leading from the garage to the mudroom. It was too early to go to bed, so Fletcher decided to sit up and listen to music. He had complied a collection of jazz and R & B records dating from the 1940s, as well as a few recorded in the 1930s by lesser known singers and musicians. To date he had a collection of more than one hundred vinyl records. Louis Armstrong, Dexter Gordon, Duke Ellington and Bessie Smith were his personal jazz favorites. Otis Redding, Ben E. King and Aretha Franklin were his R & B preferences.

Twenty minutes later, Fletcher lay on a chaise in the semidark space he had set up as an entertainment/family room. The upbeat rhythm of Benny Goodman's "Sing, Sing, Sing" flowed throughout the first story. He rested his head on folded arms and allowed himself to be swept up with his favorite music genre. It was after ten when he finally turned off the component and climbed the staircase to his bedroom. His father was scheduled to take the next two days off, which meant he had to open and close the garage.

Fletcher got into bed and spent the next half hour staring up at the ceiling as images of what he'd shared with Nicole flooded his mind like frames of a film. He turned over and pounded the pillow under his head and began slowly counting until Morpheus swallowed him whole in a deep, dreamless sleep.

Chapter Nine

"Luke, you have to wear your rain boots."

"Do I have to, Auntie?"

Nicole rolled her eyes. "Yes. Take off your sneakers and put them in your backpack." Luke turned on his heel and stomped up the staircase to his bedroom to change his footwear. It was late Saturday morning and she, Daniel, Luke and Othello were going to Fletcher's house to spend the weekend.

The weather had changed with a cold rain that had been falling without letup for the past three days. People were complaining about the rain and absence of sunlight even though they were aware the region had had an abnormally hot and dry summer season.

She shook her head in exasperation. Her nephews had spent the past two weekends with their maternal grandparents and whenever they returned, she'd noticed a difference in their behavior. They appeared angry, aggressive and were now challenging her whenever she asked them to do something. She didn't know what was going on in the Clarke household, but Nicole planned to alert the boys' counselors to identify the underlying cause or causes before she spoke to Johnnie Clarke.

The holiday had shortened the workweek for her, but it hadn't slowed the increasing number of cases on her desk. She and Preston conferred every Wednesday when they examined each client's case to ascertain their priority and to identify who would represent them in court.

Nicole had represented a teenage girl arrested for shoplifting from the drugstore. She'd recommended the girl plead guilty because it was her first offense and asked the judge for probation and community service in lieu of sixty days in the county jail. The judge had agreed and Nicole had cautioned the young woman if she did not keep the commitment to complete one hundred hours at The Falls' church's outreach food bank and check in with her probation officer once a week, she would be remanded to jail.

Preston had maintained his father's policy of not accepting clients charged with felony murder or manslaughter. The firm's focus was family law and misdemeanor charges, unlike the Miami firm where Nicole had worked as an associate. Many of their high-profile clients had been charged with white-collar crimes, drug trafficking, justifiable homicide, and some with purported acts of terrorism. The clients were extremely wealthy, their substantial retainers rapidly depleted with ongoing billable hours.

Nicole liked and enjoyed working with Preston because he treated her as an equal and not a newbie the Miami partners pressured to increase billable hours. They'd paid her well, but at the cost of working an average of sixty-plus hours a week. There were occasions when she'd had to cancel an outing with her parents because she'd been too exhausted to leave her home.

"I have on my boots, Aunt Nikki."

She smiled at Luke in a pair of olive green rain boots. "Good. Now, where's your brother?"

"He's still getting dressed."

"Please go and tell him to hurry up." Nicole had walked Othello after she'd slipped on his boots to keep his paws dry and from tracking mud into the house.

Luke walked halfway up the staircase. "Danny!" he shouted. "We're downstairs waiting for you!"

Nicole shook her head at the same time she closed her eyes. She'd lectured her nephews the only time they were to yell in the house was during an emergency. She hadn't spent any appreciable time with a lot of children before assuming the full-time responsibility of caring for her nephews, but if she were to have children of her own, she now knew what to expect.

Daniel bounded down the stairs in a pair of navy blue rain boots and a matching slicker, dragging a backpack. It bumped down each stair. "Ready!"

Nicole armed the security system and then opened the door. "Let's go, troops."

She'd remotely started the Pathfinder's engine and her nephews and Othello were in their places when she got in behind the wheel.

Tapping Fletcher's number on the screen, she said, "We're on our way," when his greeting echoed through the vehicle. She disconnected the call and backed out of the driveway. She'd loaded the SUV with one of Othello's beds, his bowls for food and water, and several cans of wet and a bag of dry food, as well as her and her nephews' overnight bags.

Nicole and Fletcher had gone back and forth about spending Saturday night at his place, but had finally reached a decision after he'd agreed to accompany them to church for services. Melissa, a devoted worshipper, had insisted her children accompany her, and out of respect for her late sister-in-law, Nicole continued the tradition.

Fletcher stood on the porch, smiling when he saw Nicole's car turn into the driveway. Reaching for a golf umbrella, he opened it and came down off the porch to shield the occupants of the SUV from the driving rain.

Luke and Daniel had put up the hoods on their slickers. Nicole wore a bright yellow poncho, matching wellies and had covered her hair with a black baseball cap. His smile grew wider when he saw Othello wearing rain boots.

"Welcome," he called out. "Everyone go inside through the garage and leave your rain gear in the mudroom." He held the umbrella over Nicole's head.

"I need to get stuff out of the cargo area," she said.

"I'll bring everything in."

Fletcher waited until everyone had gone into the house before unloading the rear of the Pathfinder. It took two trips before he closed the hatch and went inside the house. He found Nicole in the mudroom as she and the young boys had taken off their rain gear. Reaching for a towel on a stack in a wicker basket, he dried off

Othello, who braced his front paws on his chest while attempting to lick him.

"Sit, Othello," Nicole ordered and the dog obediently sat.

"I'm going to take the bags up to the bedrooms while you guys make yourselves comfortable," Fletcher said after he'd finished drying off the dog.

"Can I see where I'm going to sleep, Uncle Fletcher?" Daniel asked.

"Me, too?" Luke questioned.

Fletcher nodded. "Of course. Come with me."

He led the boys up the back staircase to the second story and into the bedroom with the twin beds. "This will be your room. You have your own bathroom, so you'll have to take turns when it comes to showering."

Luke walked over to the fireplace and peered up the chimney. "Does this work?"

"Yes. It's heated with gas."

"That's so cool," Luke whispered.

"What's cool is the firepit uses wood," Fletcher said as he walked to the window overlooking the patio and the rear of the property. He pointed when the boys joined him. "I covered it because of the rain, but if it stops by tomorrow, we'll roast marshmallows and make s'mores." Two pairs of clear round light brown eyes stared up at him. There was no doubt he had impressed them when he'd said "roast marshmallows."

"How about popcorn?" Daniel asked.

"That, too," Fletcher confirmed. "So let's hope the rain will stop before we have movie night."

Luke shared a look with his older brother. "Are we going to the movies tonight?"

Fletcher rested a hand on his head. "Yes, we are. Saturdays are always movie nights at the Austen house. I have some movies on hand for my nieces and nephews who are about your age, so when we go downstairs to the family room, you'll have to let me know what you'd like to see. As soon as you put your shoes on, you can come on down."

Fletcher walked past Nicole's bedroom to find her unpacking her bag and placing clothes in a drawer of the dresser. He retreated and stuck his head through the doorway. "I'll be downstairs if you need me."

Her head popped up and she gave him a warm smile. "I'm good here. I'll be down as soon as I put everything away and check to see if the boys have done the same."

He forced himself not to stare at her body in a pair of skinny jeans and matching stretchy top. "They're all right, Nikki. You can check on them later."

Her eyebrows shot up. "Is that your way of telling me to stop being a helicopter auntie?"

Fletcher winked at her. "Something like that."

"If that's the case, then you can take care of all the boys this weekend, and that includes Othello, and I'll just be the chaperone."

"That will definitely work. You kick back and relax while the man takes over."

"I'm hope I don't regret this."

"You won't, sweetheart. I bought everything I need to make fajitas for lunch, so can have your pick of steak, chicken or shrimp."

"I think I'm going to like hanging out here."

"Mi casa es su casa," he said.

"You won't say that if you find us living with you every other weekend," Nicole teased.

"That's where you're wrong. Sometimes it gets a

little too quiet living here alone. I'd thought about getting a dog, but I'm not certain which breed I want. I just might come over and dognap Othello for a couple of days before bringing him back."

Nicole closed a drawer and then opened another one. "You can borrow him every once in a while, now that you are best buds."

With the exception of working at the garage and interacting with folks at the Wolf Den a couple of times a month, he had begun to wonder if was mentally healthy for him to spend so much time alone. He enjoyed restoring cars and listening to music, but was that enough? He'd dated a few women since he'd left the military, none whom had ever slept with him under his roof. Fletcher had invited one to join him when he'd hosted a backyard gathering for some of the soldiers he occasionally got together with on Military Monday, but she'd been disappointed once it ended and he'd driven her back to her house.

His home had become his sanctuary—a place he coveted—and he hadn't wanted a revolving door of women coming and going. Wickham Falls' social mores were much more relaxed now than when his grandparents had been alive, but it was still a small town where gossip traveled faster than the spark of a lit fuse. And, once it became widespread, the details were so negatively altered they didn't remotely match the original chatter.

"If you're going to bring Othello over, then I'll buy everything he'll need so you don't have to haul around his food, bowls and bed."

"Remember I said borrow, not keep, Fletcher."

He winked. "I'll see you downstairs."

* * *

Nicole watched as her nephews devoured the fajitas as if they hadn't eaten in days. She had to acknowledge the marinated thinly sliced skirt steak and chicken breasts and jumbo Gulf shrimp, grilled to perfection with onions, green and sweet peppers, and folded into warm flour tortillas, surpassed any she had eaten in a number of restaurants. Fletcher had showed her a binder filled with recipes he'd gotten off the internet. Some he had attempted, but there were many more on his to-do list.

"These are so good," Daniel mumbled with a mouthful of chicken.

"Yup," his brother agreed.

Nicole lowered her eyes. She'd tried to teach them not to talk with their mouths filled with food and had failed miserably. There were just certain behaviors she could not change and she'd decided it wasn't worth the effort to continue to talk to them about it.

Fletcher, flanked by the two boys on the bench seat in the eat-in kitchen, gently patted Daniel's back. "Easy there, champ. If you talk with food in your mouth and choke on it, then I'll have to apply the Heimlich maneuver to dislodge it."

"What's a hemlick, Uncle Fletcher?" Luke asked.

Fletcher touched his napkin to the corners of his mouth. "It's a first-aid procedure used to dislodge foreign objects from the upper airway."

Daniel stared up at him. "How do you do that?"

"I'll show you later. Meanwhile, chew your food thoroughly and swallow before you talk."

"Does it hurt?" Luke questioned.

"Choking and not being able to breathe hurts. One time, when I was about your age, my brother and I were fooling around at the dinner table and my mother told us to stop. I opened my mouth to tell her it wasn't my fault, but I had a mouthful of food. I started to choke, and peas and carrots came out of my nose and mouth. Not only did my throat hurt, but the inside of my nose was sore for days. My mother never had to tell me not to talk with my mouth filled with food again."

"Wow!" the boys said in unison.

Nicole turned her head so they wouldn't see her smile of supreme satisfaction. There was no doubt Fletcher's choking episode resonated with them. Picking up the glass of sweet tea, she took a sip and gave Fletcher a barely perceptible nod.

She rested a hand over her belly. "I think I ate too much."

Fletcher slumped against the back of the bench. "You're not the only guilty one."

Luke covered his mouth with a hand to smother a yawn. "I need a nap."

"Me, too," Daniel said, also yawning. "Can we take a nap, Aunt Nikki?"

Nicole glanced at the clock on the microwave. It was a few minutes after one, but with the rain and overcast skies, it appeared much later. "Yes."

The two boys slid off the bench and walked out of the kitchen.

Fletcher smiled across the table at her. "Are you also ready for a nap?"

"I could use one, but I'm going to pass. If I nap in the afternoon, then I'm really disorientated for the rest of the day."

"What do you want to do?"

She angled her head. "That all depends on you. What do you do to relax when you're not working on your cars?"

"I read or listen to music."

Nicole put her elbow on the table and rested her chin on a fist. She hadn't known what she'd expected him to say, but it wasn't reading. Watching sports, but definitely not opening a book.

Fletcher stood and began clearing the table. She pushed back her chair and came to her feet to assist him.

"I noticed you have quite a few books about business in your office."

"Those were from some of my college courses," Fletcher explained. "It took a while, but I finally was able to earn an online undergraduate business degree. I did it more for my mother than myself, because I really didn't need it if I was going to eventually take over the business from Pop once he retires. Mom was the first one in her family to go to college, and she wanted the same for her children. I disappointed her when I turned down the athletic scholarship to enlist in the army, so the pressure fell on my brother and sister."

Fletcher scraped and rinsed dishes while Nicole stacked them in the dishwasher. "Did they disappoint her?"

"Nah. Sean graduated with a degree in chemical engineering and Charlene outdid both of us by earning a graduate and postgraduate degree in English. She's always been an overachiever."

Nicole heard the pride in Fletcher's voice when he talked about his siblings. "Would you insist that your kids go to college?"

Fletcher's hands stilled as he turned to face her. "That's something I can't answer at this time. The one thing I don't want to do is pressure them to become what I want for them. A degree definitely has more earning power than a high school diploma, but not everyone is college material. Pop has earned three times more money than Mom even if she hadn't given up her career as a social worker."

"That's because he's a business owner. And you know social workers and teachers are usually underpaid for their work."

"How about you, Nikki? Would you insist your kids go to college?"

It suddenly struck Nicole that she and Fletcher were talking about children as if both were parents. "How did we go from talking about relaxing to us having kids?"

Fletcher gave her a direct stare. "I don't know. Now, back to music. What's your favorite genre?"

"Old-school R & B."

"That's my girl!" He smiled. "As soon as we're finished here, I'll show you my record collection."

"Don't you mean CDs?"

"No, beautiful. Vinyl records."

Nicole felt pinpricks of heat dot her cheeks and she wondered if Fletcher was aware of his glibly spoken endearments: babe, sweetheart and beautiful. And she felt beautiful *and* desirable whenever they were together.

Although she had spent half her life around men, it was her career that had taken precedence over a love life. Many of her fellow female officers had fallen in love, married and had families of their own, while Nicole had allowed herself to get involved with a married man who'd used her as his sounding board, and that had threatened to derail her military career. She had continued to choose unwisely with the two men she'd dated after moving to Miami, and then had closed herself off emotionally when they had accused her of being cold, unfeeling and insensitive.

However, she found Fletcher different because he did not need her and because they had a lot more in common than she'd had with other men. They'd both been born and raised in the same town and served in the military, and had come back to Wickham Falls to support family members.

"How many records do you have?"

He dried his hands on a terry dish towel. "Come with me and I'll show you."

Fletcher couldn't help but laugh as Nicole's jaw dropped when he opened the doors under the entertainment unit in the family room to reveal countless vinyl records in their original jackets and even more CDs in jewel cases.

He sat on the floor, easing her down beside him, and handed her a record featuring the Dave Brubeck Quartet. "I collect old jazz and R & B records."

Nicole read the back of the jacket. "I remember my mother talking about the music that was popular when she was in college. She said the jukebox in the restaurant where they hung out never switched certain records because they were favorites. I remember her playing Brubeck's 'Take Five' and Louis Armstrong's 'What a Wonderful World.'"

Fletcher smiled. "My favorite of his is 'A Kiss to Build a Dream On.' There's something about his voice that's magical."

Nicole rested her head on his shoulder. "Will you play it for me?"

He thumbed through the albums he had set up in alphabetical order by artist and found the one that listed the song. Standing, he turned on the stereo system and placed the record on the turntable. Extending his hand, Fletcher stared down at Nicole, who was looking up at him.

"Come and dance with me." She placed her palm on his hand and he gently eased her up from the floor. Wrapping an arm around her waist, he pulled her flush against his body and lost himself in the words of the love song and the warmth and sweet scent of the woman in his arms.

Fletcher had admitted to Nicole that he had waited a little more than seventeen years to kiss her, but he had also waited just that long to dance with her. He had told himself when he'd driven up to her house the morning she was scheduled to go to court that he was over her rejection. He'd known that wasn't true when she'd looked at him as if he were a stranger instead of someone she'd known all her life.

She had given him the same look whenever they'd worked together on the school yearbook—that look that said he wasn't in her social class and therefore she would never agree to date him.

Now that he'd kissed her and held her in his arms, Fletcher knew the wait had been more than worth it. They danced, barely moving their feet as he buried his face in her hair and inhaled a whiff of coconut clinging to the short strands. Everything about her was soft and feminine, and in that instant he knew he was falling in love with Nicole. He realized *love* was a strong word, but he could not explain away the depth of the feelings he had for her. His head dipped and he pressed his mouth to her ear. He had memorized the words to the poignant love song and he felt her stiffen as he whispered them, before she relaxed again against his chest.

Fletcher not only wanted a kiss to build a dream on with Nicole, he also wanted so much more. He wanted her to share his life and their future. But that would only be possible if she agreed to come home to Wickham Falls. She'd told him her home was now in Miami, Florida, and she was not involved with anyone, which meant she had nothing keeping her from relocating. He was certain she wouldn't have a problem selling her house, and if she wanted to continue practicing law, she already had a position with Preston McAvoy.

He knew he had to be patient with Nicole and not broach the subject or to put undue pressure on her about her upcoming plans. It was September and he still had at least four, maybe even five, months to subtly convince her to stay.

"What are you doing, Fletcher?" she whispered as he trailed light kisses down the column of her neck.

"Seeing if you taste as good as you look."

She giggled. "What's your verdict?"

Fletcher pressed a soft kiss to her forehead. "You are delicious." Leaning back slightly, he saw her smile. "Your eyes are the pieces they put in chocolate chip cookies." He punctuated his words with a kiss over each eyelid. "Your nose reminds me of the peak on a miniature macaroon, and your lips are as sweet and soft as meringue."

"You make it sound as if I'm quite a confection," she teased, her smile becoming a wide grin.

Fletcher stared at her under lowered lids. "You just don't know the half of it, Nikki. Whether you realize it or not, you're the total package."

Her expression changed like quicksilver as a slight frown appeared between her eyes. "Don't, Fletcher."

His frown matched hers, deepening with each passing second. "Don't what, Nicole? Don't say what I feel," he said, not giving her the chance to answer his question.

She pushed against his chest. "You don't know what you're saying. I can't give you whatever you want."

"How do you know what I want?" he countered.

"You want something I'm unable to give you."

"And what is that?" Fletcher asked, enunciating each word.

"You want me to stay."

He swore under his breath, wondering if she was that perceptive or he that transparent. "And you don't want to?"

Nicole shook her head. "It's not that I don't want to, but I can't. I have a life in Florida and—"

"A life?" he asked, interrupting her. "Didn't you tell me that you have to look for employment once you get back? What if you can't find something you like?"

Her eyes narrowed, reminding him of a cat about to pounce. "Do you know how selfish you sound, Fletcher? How can you think you know what's best for me? I may not have a job, but that doesn't mean I don't have options. If I can't find a position with a firm and a salary commensurate with my education and experience, then I can always apply to the Miami-Dade State Attorney's Office. So don't think I'm a one-trick pony."

Suddenly, Fletcher felt as if he had come down with a serious case of foot-in-mouth. He hadn't meant to belittle her ability to take care of herself; all he wanted was to love and protect her.

"I'm sorry, Nikki. I shouldn't have said what I said. Will you forgive me?"

The seconds ticked by before her expression softened and her lips parted in a smile. "Yes, I forgive you." Reaching up, she placed her hand on his cheek. "You have to remember you're no longer Special Forces and I don't need saving."

Fletcher ran his forefinger down the length of her nose. "Can't you allow me to put on my cape and play superhero once or twice?"

"Aquaman doesn't wear a cape."

"Maybe I should see the movie to find out if I even like him."

"Oh, you'll like him, Fletcher."

Taking her hand, he led her to the oversize chaise and seated her. He folded his body down and pulled her into his arms. "I need you to put the brakes on me whenever I get carried away and try to run your life."

Nicole snuggled closer. "All I have to do is pull rank and that should stop you, Sergeant Austen."

He kissed the top of her head. "That's not fair, Captain Campos."

"Haven't you heard life's not fair?"

"Please don't remind me. That was my mother's favorite phrase whenever she wouldn't let me do something and I told her she wasn't fair."

Nicole laughed. "My mother used to say the same thing." She paused. "Do you think that's a mama thing?"

"It has to be," Fletcher said as he closed his eyes.

The gentle splash of rain tapping on the windows, the melodic sound of the trumpet and the soft curves of Nicole molded to him, lulled Fletcher into a state of total relaxation. Now, if she were to ask him what he did to relax, he would have to admit having her with him was fundamental.

Chapter Ten

"Yes, Miss Pratt?"

The buzzing of the office intercom shattered Nicole's concentration. She was scheduled to attend a court hearing the following morning to defend her shoplifting client who'd violated probation. The young woman had only completed ten of her mandated one hundred hours of community service, and she had been arrested again for breaking into a neighbor's house and taking off with a laptop computer.

"There's someone up front with a delivery for you."

Nicole massaged her forehead with her fingertips. "I'll get it later, so please sign it for me."

"I think you better come up and see it for yourself."

Nicole bit down on her lip in frustration. When she'd come in earlier that morning she had instructed Marlena Pratt to hold her calls, telling her that she couldn't see anyone because she had to put together a defense to keep an eighteen-year-old client from going to jail—a client who denied having a substance-abuse problem.

"Okay, I'm coming." She walked out of her office and down the hall to the reception area. The deliveryman from the local florist held a vase with a large bouquet of red and white long-stemmed roses.

"The vase is heavy, Miss Campos. After you sign the receipt, I'll carry it to your office."

"Who sent you flowers, Nicole?" Miss Pratt asked, peering over her half-glasses.

Nicole deliberately ignored the older woman. Nothing went on in the office that the receptionist was not aware of. She would occasionally overstep her responsibility as office manager, while Preston held off reprimanding her because of her blind loyalty to his father, and now to him.

She signed the receipt, removed the small envelope off the colorful cellophane and slipped it into the pocket of her slacks. "I don't know."

Miss Pratt stood behind the reception partition. "Why don't you read it?"

Nicole smiled at the deliveryman. "Please come with me and I'll show you where to put the vase." She retreated to her office, him following, and removed a bill from her handbag. "You can leave it on the credenza." She handed him a tip. "Thank you."

He inclined his head. "Thank you, Miss Campos."

Waiting until he left the office, Nicole closed the door, pulled the envelope out of her pocket and read the card.

Thank you for a wonderful weekend. We must do it again!
JFA

Pressing her palms together, she brought her fingers to her mouth. Fletcher had sent her flowers to thank her for the weekend, when she should've been the one thanking him. The weather had conspired to keep them indoors and they'd passed the time listening to music, playing board games, cooking together and watching movies. She and Fletcher had stayed up past midnight to binge-watch *Ray Donovan*.

The rain had slackened off to a steady drizzle when they'd left to go to church. She had not missed the whispers when she'd walked in with Fletcher and her nephews; it was the first time they were seen together in public. Fletcher had surprised Luke and Daniel when, instead of driving to his house, he told them they were going to Ruthie's for Sunday brunch. The family-style all-you-can-eat buffet restaurant was a favorite for locals who opted out of the tradition of serving Sunday dinner.

Sitting and reaching for her cell, she tapped his number.

"Should I assume you got them?"

Nicole smiled. "What happened to hello or good afternoon?" she teased.

His chuckle caressed her ear. "I much prefer a kiss good-night."

Heat flooded her face when she recalled the stolen passionate kisses they'd shared whenever they were certain the boys were asleep. Fletcher holding and kissing her conjured up old and new sensations.

"You're going to have to wait on that," she said quietly into the mouthpiece. "I called to thank you for the flowers. They're incredibly beautiful."

"Beautiful flowers for a beautiful woman. And please don't tell me I'm good for your ego."

Nicole pantomimed zipping her mouth even though Fletcher couldn't see her. "Done."

"Good. What's on your calendar today, Counselor?"

"I'm working on my argument to defend a client who violated probation."

"When are you scheduled to appear in court?"

"Tomorrow."

"I'm certain you're going get him or her off."

Nicole smiled. "Thanks for the vote of confidence."

"You don't need it, babe. Whatever happens, don't forget I'm here to lend a shoulder or we can celebrate with a bottle of bubbly."

"I'll be certain to let you know the outcome. By the way, I only called to thank you for the flowers."

"You're welcome, and I'm going to hang up because I know you're busy. Do you mind if I call you later tonight?"

"Of course not, Fletcher."

"Later, babe."

Fletcher hung up and Nicole ended the call. She stared at the decorative hand-painted vase cradling at least two dozen roses. It was the second time he had sent her flowers. The first bouquet was delivered to the house, and now her office. It was as if he was silently announcing to her coworkers that they were involved with each other. And she knew before the day was over that Preston and the paralegals would know she'd received a bouquet of flowers from an admirer—an admirer who had unknowingly sneaked under her wall to keep all men at a distance because she'd felt at this time in her life she didn't want or need them.

But Jesse Fletcher Austen had proved her wrong. He'd won her, Daniel, Luke and Othello over just being himself. Not only did she want him, she also needed him. She needed Fletcher to fill up the empty hours when she wasn't caring for her nephews or reviewing client files. He was good to and for her, and she hoped she was the same for him.

Nicole sat across the table from her client and struggled not to lose her temper. She had spent hours interviewing Sheryl Lynn Dixon and it was the first time she'd admitted to having a drug problem. She glared at the teenager with her wealth of dirty-blond hair and large dark green eyes framed by a double set of black lashes.

"I'd asked you over and over whether you were using drugs and you said no. Your parents hired me to defend you. How do you expect me to do that when you lie to me? If your family hadn't taken out a loan for my firm to represent you, I'd walk away and let the judge send you to jail. And now instead of facing sixty days, it might be a year."

Tears filled Sheryl Lynn's eyes and streamed down her face. She attempted to wipe them away but her right wrist was handcuffed to the table. "I can't go to jail, Miss Campos. My mama's cancer came back and she needs me."

Nicole wanted to tell her client she should've thought of that before burglarizing her neighbor's home to get money to buy drugs. "I'm going to do everything I can to keep you out of jail, but you have to promise me that you're going to do exactly what I'm going to ask the court, otherwise you'll finding yourself looking for another attorney." She glared at Sheryl Lynn. "Do you understand what I'm saying?"

"Yes, ma'am."

"When was the last time you used?"

"Two days ago."

"Good. I'll see you in the courtroom." Nicole rose and nodded to the court officer standing near the door. "Thank you," she said when he opened it for her.

Nicole stood next her client, her eyes trained on the director of probation entering the courtroom through the doorway that led to the judge's chambers. His appearance did not bode well for Sheryl Lynn, who still wore the jail-issued jumpsuit. "I don't want you to say a word until I tell you." The younger woman nodded.

The prosecutor from the DA's office introduced the charges against Sheryl Lynn, recommending she be remanded to prison to serve out her sentence on the prior charge along with an additional two years for the burglary.

Nicole stared straight ahead when she heard Sheryl Lynn's father gasp from where he sat on the bench behind her. There was no way she was going to allow her client to spend three years in prison for nonviolent misdemeanors. "Your Honor, I'd like my client to be drug tested."

The elderly judge leaned forward. "Here? Now?"

She nodded. "Yes, Your Honor. My client is addicted to drugs and, as such, shouldn't be in jail but mandated to a treatment program. Her mother's cancer has returned and she'll need Miss Dixon to care for her when she undergoes her chemotherapy treatments."

"Miss Dixon, are you currently taking drugs?" the judge questioned.

Sheryl Lynn stood. "Yes, Your Honor."

"And you agree to have someone test you?"

"Yes, Your Honor."

The judge banged his gavel. "We'll have a twenty-minute recess while the defendant is drug tested."

Nicole watched a female court officer lead Sheryl Lynn out of the courtroom. Her client had lied to her once and she prayed she was telling the truth about her drug use. If she came up with a positive toxicology, she would be mandated treatment in lieu of incarceration. She also would have to complete her community service hours and meet with her probation officer.

Sheryl Lynn was led back into the courtroom as an officer handed the judge a sheet a paper. Nicole squeezed the girl's hand before he revealed the results of the test. She'd tested positive for cannabis, opiates and crack cocaine.

Judge Shelton stared at Sheryl Lynn. "It looks as if you've dodged a bullet, Miss Dixon, because you were on your way to jail.

"I'm mandating you to an outpatient treatment program for the next year, where you will be subjected to random drug testing. If any of them come back dirty, it doesn't matter what is going on in your private life because you *will* go to jail. You will continue with your community service and check in weekly with your parole officer to let him know when you're scheduled to take your mother for her therapy. He will give you a curfew and make unannounced home visits. So, it's up to you, Miss Dixon, whether you're ready to comply with the dictates of this court."

"I am, Your Honor."

"Miss Campos, I suggest you assist your client in enrolling in treatment ASAP."

Nicole nodded, smiling. "I will, Your Honor."

"Miss Dixon, you've been given a second chance, so take advantage of it." He banged his gavel. "This case is closed."

Nicole turned and smiled at Mr. Dixon, who gripped her hands in gratitude. "You'll be able to take her home as soon as the paperwork for her release is completed."

"How can I thank you, Miss Campos?"

"Thank me by driving your daughter directly to the Wickham Falls drug counseling center for an evaluation. She'll need all of your support to help her through this crisis."

Nicole felt sorry for the man who now had to deal with his wife's disease *and* his daughter's addiction. West Virginia, along with many states, was in the grip of an opiate epidemic, and treatment, not incarceration, had become a priority.

He nodded. "I will."

Nicole left the courthouse and got into her car. She sat staring through the windshield without starting it up. Defending a client with a history of substance abuse had come too close to home for her.

Reggie had denied over and over that he was abusing his pain meds, until he wasn't able to get out of bed to care for his sons. The one time he'd answered the phone and was totally incoherent, Nicole had known something was wrong and immediately booked a flight to West Virginia.

Her instincts were proved right when she'd driven up to discover Reggie so high he initially did not recognize her. However, in a moment of lucidity, she did get him to agree to sign the documents giving her temporary custodial custody and power of attorney of his finances.

Nicole started up the SUV and tapped Preston's private

number on the navigation screen. "I have good news," she said once he answered the call.

"You got her off?"

"Not entirely. She's not going to jail." She told him everything about her pretrial conversation with Sheryl Lynn and the judge's mandate about treatment.

"Nice work, Nicole. I've been seriously thinking of asking you to come on full-time as a partner."

Nicole grimaced. "I'm honored you've asked, but you know I can't accept your offer."

"You don't have to give me your answer now."

"But I just did give you my answer, Preston." Her boss had dropped hints about making her a junior partner and, although flattered, Nicole knew she could not accept his offer.

"It is possible that you will change your mind."

"No, Preston. It is not possible."

"Well, you can't blame me for asking."

"If you don't mind, I'd like to take the rest of the afternoon off."

"Take the rest of the week off, Nicole."

Nicole smiled. "Are you sure the office won't fall apart without me?" she teased.

"We'll try to hold it down until you come back Monday."

"I'll stop by to drop off Sheryl Lynn's file—"

"Take it home with you, Nicole. And don't forget to have some fun."

Nicole disconnected the call, shifted into gear and drove out of the parking lot. Preston had suggested she have fun and that was what she intended to do. After Daniel and Luke boarded the bus tomorrow morning, she planned to go back to bed and sleep until late morning—something she hadn't done in a while.

She arrived home, changed into jogging clothes and took Othello for a run. By the time Nicole returned to the house, showered and prepared a salad for her lunch, the bus had dropped off her nephews.

"Aunt Nikki, do we have to go back to counseling?"

Nicole's hand halted cutting circles on the sheet of cookie dough. She stared at Daniel and Luke sitting in the nook. It was their favorite spot to do homework after dinner.

"Why don't you want to go back, Daniel?"

"I get tired of talking about the same thing."

"Me, too," Luke said in agreement.

It had been two months since her nephews had started seeing counselors for weekly individual sessions, and their therapists had reported they were adjusting to the loss of their mother and their father's absence.

"I'll call your therapists tomorrow to ask them whether they believe you're ready to stop coming." Her answer appeared to satisfy them when they nodded and went back to doing homework. Nicole wondered if it was something both wanted, or if Daniel was the one who did not want to go.

When she'd questioned their counselors about the boys' aggressiveness whenever they'd spent time with their grandparents, they contradicted her concern with the explanation that her nephews were competing with their cousins for their grandparents' attention. Their grandmother, in particular, who tended to be overindulgent with her grandchildren.

A smile parted her lips as she stared at the two boys writing in their notebooks. When Reggie had informed her that she was going to become an aunt, Nicole had done a happy dance. Even before Daniel was born she'd begun purchasing items for a layette. And the first time she'd held the three-month-old baby in her arms and he'd given her a crooked smile, her heart melted. Luke came along two years later and Nicole had asked Reggie and Melissa to add a codicil to their will, listing her as legal guardian in the event anything happened to them. Little had she known at the time that Melissa would lose her life and Reggie would be unable to care for them because of substance abuse.

She finished cutting the circles of buttery shortbread dough, placing them on a parchment-lined cookie sheet. Nicole topped some with crushed pecans, colorful sprinkles, chopped dried cherries and cranberries. She baked a new batch of cookies every two weeks, much to the delight of her nephews. Peanut butter, oatmeal raisin and chocolate chip were among their favorites. She placed the two cookie sheets in the oven and set the timer.

Luke closed his notebook and gathered his pencils. "I'm finished, Auntie Nikki."

Her eyes caressed his round brown face with its sparkling light brown eyes. "Do you want me to check it?"

"No, thank you. I'm going to bed now." He came over and hugged her. "Good night."

Nicole no longer had to remind the boys to brush their teeth before going to bed. She dropped a kiss on his head. "Good night, sweetie."

Daniel groaned as he erased whatever he'd written.

"Do you need help with something?"

"Nah, I'm good. I added something wrong."

It was a rare occasion that her nephews asked her to help them with their homework, although she wanted them to know they could always approach her with something they did not understand.

Daniel slid off the bench seat. "I'm finished with math and spelling, and I'm going upstairs to review for my social studies test."

Nicole hugged him. "Good night." She knew there would come a time when they wouldn't feel comfortable with her overt affection, but she intended to hug and kiss them until they told her to stop.

The cookies were cooling on a rack when her cell rang and Fletcher's name appeared on the display. "Hey," she crooned.

"Hey yourself. Do you need a shoulder or bubbly?"

"Both. Come on over and I'll tell you."

"I'll see you in about twenty minutes."

"I'll leave the door unlocked, so just let yourself in."

"Do you think that's wise, Nikki? It's not the past when folks in The Falls didn't lock their doors or cars."

"Don't forget, I have Othello. Anyone crazy enough to break in will get the surprise of their life."

Fletcher laughed. "I rest my case."

Fletcher opened the outer door and then the beveled-glass inner one and was greeted by Othello. He rested his free hand on the dog's head. "How's it going, boy?" He still was awed how easily he'd bonded with the powerful canine. Turning, he locked both doors.

"Something smells delicious," he announced, walking into the kitchen to find Nicole filling a large glass jar with cookies.

She smiled at him. “I just baked a batch of cookies for the boys. Whenever they come home from school, they have a couple with a glass of milk. Do you want to sample a few?”

It had been two days since he’d last seen Nicole, but to Fletcher it appeared to be a lot longer. She was the first woman, other than his sister, to sleep under his roof, and he wanted her to be the last. Not only had he enjoyed every moment they’d been together, he’d found her nephews to be bright, engaging and unbelievably well-adjusted given the loss of their mother and their father’s absence.

He’d been filled with pride when escorting them into church and overhearing people refer to them as a nice family. Nicole and her nephews were family. He’d just assumed the role as a temporary dad until Reggie’s return.

Fletcher set the bag with a bottle of chilled champagne on the countertop. Nicole’s bare, flawless face, large, bright eyes and the narrow headband holding her bangs off her forehead made her appear much younger than she was. Just looking at her, one would never have suspected she had seen her share of combat as a helicopter pilot. And the revealing white tank top and black leggings sent his libido into overdrive.

He’d successfully repressed his sexual urges when with her because he did not want to face the reality that he wanted to sleep with Nicole. He wanted her for more than sex. He had found her so easy to talk to, and there was never a time when he felt as if he had to censor himself. That was not to say he’d had not his share of faux pas, but he was mature enough to apologize.

“Yes, please. Where are the boys?”

"They're upstairs. Luke is probably in bed asleep, while Daniel will turn in around ten."

"Do you have to fight with them to go to bed?"

Nicole shook her head. "No. I used to have a problem getting them up in the morning because they stay up late whenever there's no school. I bought both digital alarm clocks and programmed them to go off at the same time Monday through Friday. The clocks aren't on the nightstands, where they can reach over and hit the snooze button, so if they don't want to hear the alarm, they have to get out of bed to turn it off."

Fletcher smiled. "Whatever works."

She pointed to the bag. "Did you bring a corkscrew?"

"Yes, ma'am." He removed the bottle, two flutes, a corkscrew and, with a minimum effort, removed the cork.

"I like a man who comes prepared," Nicole said as he filled the flutes with the pale bubbly wine.

"I was a Boy Scout and our motto was Be Prepared."

"I do remember you wearing your Scout uniform and marching with your troop during the Memorial Day parade," Nicole said as she removed two dessert plates from an overhead cabinet. "I was ticked off because we didn't have a Brownie or Girl Scout troop in The Falls."

"They had one in Mineral Springs," Fletcher reminded her.

She narrowed her eyes at him. "That wasn't going to happen because folks here didn't want to have anything to do with people from the Springs."

"That did not stop your brother from marrying one."

Nicole nodded. "No one knew he was dating Melissa on the low-low until after they'd eloped."

"Don't you mean the down low?"

"No, Fletcher. It was so clandestine it was like a CIA Black Ops."

"I suppose they had their reasons for keeping their relationship secret."

Nicole lifted bare shoulders under the tank top. "Reggie would never admit it, but I believe he thought our parents would be opposed to him marrying someone who didn't have a college degree."

"Is that what your parents told you? That you could only marry a man with a degree?"

"Of course not! My parents aren't that elitist. My father told me if I was ever going to get married, then to make certain I would be able to support our children in case something happened to my husband."

"So, you don't plan for your husband to support you and your children?"

"Don't try to put words in my mouth, Fletcher. Of course, I would like him to be able to financially support our family, but it wouldn't bother me if I had the greater earning potential. Marriage shouldn't be a power struggle about who makes more money. I've known men to give up their careers and become stay-at-home dads while their wives are the breadwinners."

"Don't you think they become resentful after a while being stuck at home with the kids while their wives socialize with clients or their coworkers?"

Nicole picked up the flute but didn't put it to her mouth. "You sound like a throwback to generations where men worked out of the house while their women were always barefoot and pregnant."

"I was just playing devil's advocate. I may be old-school when it comes to not wanting to become a father unless I'm married, but I wouldn't care if my wife made ten times more money than I did."

"What about staying home and taking care of the kids?"

"I'm definitely agreeable to taking paternity leave."

Nicole raised her flute, touching it to his. "One of these days you're going to be a wonderful husband and father for some woman."

Fletcher stared at Nicole over the rim of his glass before taking a sip. "Are you up for the position?"

Her hand came down, seemingly in slow motion, as she gave him a long, penetrating stare. "Are you proposing marriage?" Her query was barely a whisper.

Setting down his flute, Fletcher crossed his arms over the front of his sweatshirt. "I'm seriously thinking about it."

Nicole was certain Fletcher could hear and see her heart wildly pumping in her chest. She felt as if her emotions were under attack as she stared into the amber-colored orbs, making it almost impossible for her to move or breathe. She liked him—no, she more than liked him. What had begun as a girlhood crush had evolved into something Nicole did not want to admit, because it would only result in heartache when it came time to leave Fletcher. She had fallen in love with his gentleness, honesty, generosity, loyalty and masculinity, and that had her wanting to lie with him.

"You want to marry me without knowing if I love you?"

He lowered his eyes as if hiding his innermost thoughts from her. "Do you think you could love me?"

Nicole bit her lip. He'd answered her question with

a question. "I'm not saying it's impossible," she said truthfully.

He smiled and tiny lines fanned out around his eyes. "I'll accept that." Coming around the breakfast bar, Fletcher took her hand and led her into the family room. He sat on the love seat and pulled her down beside him. "I know you're going back to Florida early next year, but I don't want you to leave without knowing that I love you. I cannot and will not put pressure on you to give up your life in Miami, but just remember I'll be here if you decide to come home."

Burying her face in his shoulder, Nicole breathed in the smell of his now-familiar bodywash. "You're willing to wait for me?"

"I've waited seventeen years, so a few more shouldn't matter."

"What if I never come back?"

"Once you make that decision, I think it's only fair that you call me so we both can move on with our lives."

Nicole closed her eyes and suddenly the man she loved sounded selfish and manipulative. He had to know she had feelings for him. Otherwise she wouldn't have permitted him to kiss her with a passion that had nearly spilled over to them making love to each other. And she knew it would've happened if they had been alone in the house.

"I do love you, Fletcher. Right now, my life is in flux, so it's impossible to commit to anything beyond taking care of Luke and Daniel until Reggie comes back. Earlier today Preston asked me to join the firm as a junior partner and I had to turn him down."

What she didn't disclose to Fletcher was that one of the senior partners at the firm in Miami had sent her an email offering her a position, if and when she decided to return. It was apparent her replacement wasn't working out as well as they'd hoped. She had held off replying because she did not want to work for a company that only viewed her as a cash cow and not someone going through a family crisis.

When she'd approached the head of HR, she'd told the woman she would be willing to take an extended leave without pay and that when she returned she was willing to accept a reduction in salary, if they were willing to rehire her. It had taken less than twenty-four hours for the secretary of one of the partners to place an envelope on her desk. It contained a check for her hours worked and a two-sentence letter thanking her for her employment while hoping she was able to resolve her family problems.

"Is it something you would consider if you don't find something in Miami?"

"Yes, only because I really enjoy working for Preston. He's not about inflated retainers or gouging clients out of their hard-earned money for legal representation."

Fletcher kissed her hair. "So, you were able to win your client's case?"

"My client was given probation and has mandated drug treatment and community service in lieu of jail or maybe even prison."

"Have you ever lost a case?"

Tilting her chin, Nicole stared up at Fletcher. "No, because today was the first day I've ever had to defend someone."

His inky black eyebrows shot up. "You're kidding?"

She smiled. "No, I'm not. My role was to do research

and remain in the background while the junior and senior partners argued cases."

Dipping his head, Fletcher touched his mouth to hers as he caressed her lips until they parted under his. Nicole moaned softly when his tongue slipped into her mouth. She felt herself drowning in the sweetness of his kiss as waves of ecstasy buffeted her from head to toe. She knew if she didn't stop him, she would beg him to make love to her. Not only was it not the time but, most important, it was not the place.

"Fletcher! Please let me go." He pulled back and stared at her as if she was a stranger.

"I'm sorry, Nikki. I shouldn't have done that."

She traced his eyebrows with a finger, smoothing out the frown that had settled between his eyes. "There's no need to apologize. It's just the wrong time and place." Her explanation seemed to mollify him when he smiled.

"You're right. There will be another appropriate time and place. I think I need another drink."

They returned to the kitchen, where Nicole drank two glasses of champagne to Fletcher's three.

She teased him, saying if he were stopped for driving under the influence, she'd represent him pro bono. She filled a large plastic container with an assortment of cookies for him to take.

"Please be sure to share them with the guys at the garage."

"Yeah, right!" he drawled. "Their eyes may shine and their teeth may grit, but these here cookies they will never git."

"If you're not going to share, then I'll bake another batch and drop them off in a couple of days." Nicole patted his shoulder as she handed him the bag with corkscrew. “Go home, babe.”

He gave her a pointed look. “Are you putting me out?”

Going on tiptoe, she kissed his cheek. “Yes, because I want to call my mother before it gets too late. She’s early to bed and early to rise.”

“When am I going to see you again?”

“Friday. I’ll come over after I drop the boys off.”

“Are you bringing Othello? I bought a bed, bowls and food for him.”

“Are you suggesting we sleep over?” Nicole asked.

“Of course, sweetheart. You have to let me know if you want to go out for dinner, or if it’s not raining, then I’ll cook outdoors.”

“We can stay in Friday and then decide what we want to do for Saturday.”

Fletcher winked at her. “That sounds like a plan.”

Nicole walked him to the door, watching on the porch until he got into his car and backed out of the driveway. Othello stood next to her, whining softly. “It’s okay, boy. You’ll see him again in a few days.” She went back into the house, locking the doors behind her. Later that night she would let Othello out the back door for his last romp and then arm the security system before going to bed.

The day had been one of revelations. She had kept her client out of jail. Preston had offered her a partnership. Fletcher had given her an indirect marriage proposal, while offering her an out if she decided to return to live in Florida for the rest of her life.

She did love him. He had everything she’d want in a man with whom she could share her life and future. But only time would tell, the closer it came to her brother’s recovery, whether she would give up the lifestyle to which she had become accustomed in Miami to return to a rural town with its two stoplights. A town where the railroad ran through the middle of downtown, and that claimed only two eating establishments.

Nicole had come to look for the colorful lights, the beach and the infusion of Latin energy that made her feel alive after she completed a sixty-hour workweek.

"I have time to make a decision," she whispered. She emptied the remains of the champagne into the sink, rinsed the bottle and put it in a plastic bin to be recycled.

Picking up her cell phone, she called her mother and settled in to listen to Elizabeth giving her an update as to what was going on in her life and those in her gated community.

Chapter Eleven

"Hey, son, the mailman just delivered the mail and there's a package for you."

Fletcher wiped his hands on an oil-covered rag and closed the hood to the fifteen-year-old Honda. He'd had to install a new battery, replace all four tires, fan belt, intake manifold and cooling fan for the man who wanted to give his granddaughter her first car. The sedan's body was in good shape, while some of the parts had needed to be replaced.

He stared at his father standing in the doorway to the office. "I'll be right there." Fletcher motioned to Billy Grimes, who'd just finished an oil change. "You can take it out now." Walking over the sink in a corner of the garage, he washed his hands with a special soap and scrubbed his nails with a small brush.

Jesse sat in the worn leather recliner, watching a

sports channel. He pointed to the box. "It's from the judge's daughter."

Fletcher met a pair of eyes so much like his own. He'd inherited his father's eye color and height, and his mother's features. "Her name is Nicole, Pop."

The older man waved a heavily veined hand. Jesse had recently complained of stiffness in the joints, and Fletcher suspected it was arthritis. "I know what her name is, but I've always called her the judge's daughter."

Fletcher picked up a box cutter, slid it along the tape, opened the box and removed a tin filled with cookies. He read the enclosed card and then handed it to his father.

"What did she send me?" Jesse questioned.

"Homemade cookies."

Jesse sat straight and swung his legs over the side of the recliner. "Word of advice, son. Don't let her go."

"She's not mine to keep, Pop."

Lines of consternation crossed Jesse's forehead. "Do you like her?"

"Of course," Fletcher said without hesitation.

"Well, what are you going to do about it?"

Fletcher's expression changed, becoming a mask of stone. "Stay out of it, Pop."

"But—"

"I mean it, Pop," Fletcher countered, cutting off his father. "What goes on between me and Nicole is not open for discussion."

Throwing back his head, Jesse laughed as if he had taken leave of his senses. He pointed to his eldest son. "That's the very same thing I said to your grandfather when he asked me about going out with your mother. And you know what happened?"

"Yeah, yeah," Fletcher drawled as he attempted not to smile. "You married her."

Jesse quickly sobered. "Yes, I married her and thirty-eight years later I'm still the happiest man in the world, because she is the best wife and mother any man could ask for."

Fletcher extended the tin. "You're becoming maudlin. Eat a cookie, Pop."

"I don't know what *maudlin* means, but I will have one." Jesse took a bite of the shortbread cookie and before finishing it, he reached for another. "These are good."

"Save some for Billy and Charles." Fletcher topped the tin and returned to the garage to share the cookies with their employees. His father had hinted about him not letting Nicole go, when he did not know what he could say or do to convince her to stay. He knew exerting pressure was not the answer, and that meant he had to let everything unfold on its own.

Othello began whining and turning around and around as soon as Nicole pulled into the driveway to Fletcher's house. She taken advantage of her days off to visit the local salon for a full-body massage, facial, manicure and pedicure. The stylist had trimmed her hair in a becoming style that framed her face to its best advantage. She had also baked another batch of cookies, stored them in an airtight tin and sent it by overnight mail to Austen Auto & Sons.

"Okay, boy. Settle down. I'll let you out in a minute." The words were barely off her tongue when Fletcher appeared, opened the hatch, and man and dog reunited as if they hadn't seen each other in months instead of days. She reached for her overnight bag on the passenger seat, handing it to Fletcher as he helped her down. He wore a bibbed apron stamped with Kiss the Cook.

"Really, Fletcher? Do you realize you're not very subtle?"

He smiled. "There's no shame in my game. I ain't too proud to beg."

Going on tiptoe, she brushed a light kiss over his mouth. "You *are* shameless."

"No, I'm not, sweetheart. I'm just a man who happens to be in love with you. And I like what you've done with your hair."

Fletcher was in love with her and she loved him, but refused to dwell on where it would lead because she did not want to think about the future, just now. And he had become her Mr. Right Now. Nicole smiled. "I'm letting it grow. If I'm going to spend the winter here, then I'm going to need longer hair to keep my head warm." Not only would she need more hair, but she also would have to wear a cap once the temperature dropped below forty because she had become accustomed to Florida's mild winters.

Fletcher wrapped his free arm around her waist and escorted her around to the rear of the house. A soft gasp escaped Nicole when she saw tiny white lights intertwined in the branches of the trees shading the patio. Strategically placed outdoor lamps illuminated the outdoor kitchen. Twilight had shrouded the landscape in glorious shadows reminiscent of a watercolor painting, and the pinpoints of emerging stars against the darkening sky was ethereal. Candles flickered under the lanterns positioned around the perimeter, and several lit citronella torches added more brightness to the outdoor space. A slight breeze stirred the wind chimes suspended from the ceiling of the rear wraparound porch.

"It's beautiful." She was unable to disguise the awe in her voice.

"Is it romantic enough for you?"

Looping her arms through Fletcher's, Nicole rested her head against his shoulder. "It's perfect."

"That's because you're perfect. I'm going to take your bag inside, then I'll bring out the food. Oh, I forgot. We got the cookies the other day. When Pop saw the card, he said he would've preferred to thank you in person."

"Did he like them?"

"Like them? That's an understatement. He ate one and then another, and I had to take the tin before he devoured every one. He was madder than a wet hen when I shared them with the other guys."

"What did you do with the ones I gave you?"

"I gave half to my mother. Mom told me she has one with her morning coffee and another with her afternoon tea. She said if you decide to sell them, she would be one of your steady customers."

"I bake cookies for fun and not profit." She had done more cooking and baking during the past three months than she had in years. "Do you need me to help you with anything?" she asked.

"No, babe. I've skewered the veggies, seasoned the steaks and chilled the wine. Just sit and relax."

Nicole watched Fletcher as he opened a pocket door and disappeared inside. She strolled around the patio, smiling. Her man had gone out of his way to transform the outdoor space into a romantic wonderland with lights and candles. He had covered a small round table with a white cloth, a quartet of lit votives in glass holders and place settings for two. Two wineglasses were turned over and the plates were covered with mesh food tents. Fletcher had suggested she relax, and that was exactly what she planned to do. She sat on a webbed recliner and smiled when Othello ambled over and lay beside the chair.

Earlier that morning she'd sent Fletcher a text message telling him she was going to feed and walk the dog before coming over. Othello must have sensed he was going out in the car when he saw the overnight bag.

"You like coming here, don't you? So do I," Nicole said, continuing with her monologue. "Tomorrow morning I'm going to let you run and chase rabbits, but you have to promise not to hurt any." Othello raised his head as if he understood what she was telling him. "There are times when I feel you need a lady friend so you can have company when I leave you alone in the house. Of course, you can't make babies because you're neutered, but if you could, I know they would be adorable. What type of lady would you like? Another Malinois or a German shepherd? You would need a big girl because you are a big boy."

"Do you always have lengthy conversations with your fur baby?"

Nicole sat straighter. Fletcher had returned carrying a cloth-covered tray. "Of course."

Fletcher set the tray on the countertop next to the sink. "Does he ever talk back?"

She slipped off the recliner and stood next to him. "I didn't know you were a comedian."

* * *

Fletcher knew he had struck a nerve with Nicole when he heard a trace of censure color her tone as her protective instincts surfaced. "I'm not trying to be funny, babe. It's just amusing to hear you talking to the dog as if he's human and understands what you're saying."

"He does understand commands. I..." Her voice trailed off abruptly. "Why are we talking about a dog, Fletcher?"

"What do you want to talk about?"

Nicole rested a hand on his back. "You."

Fletcher felt the warmth from Nicole's palm through the cotton fabric of his T-shirt as he uncovered the tray, revealing skewers of red and green pepper, cubed squash, cherry tomato, onion and mushroom. There was also a platter of rib eye steaks seasoned with kosher salt and freshly ground pepper, and a dish of sliced garlic and fresh herbs. He had come to look for her spontaneity whenever she kissed or touched him.

"What about me, love?" He smiled when her hand made circular motions on his shoulder blade.

"Do you ever see the soldiers you served with since your separation?"

Fletcher nodded. "We get together the second week in May every other year to go fishing in the Florida Keys. One of the guys bought and lives on a large fishing boat that sleeps six. We hang out in Key West for a couple of days eating and drinking until everyone arrives. We sail down to Puerto Rico and spend a few days there before coming back."

"Do you actually do any fishing?"

"Some," he admitted, smiling. "The reunion is more

about catching up on what's going on in our lives than seeing who can catch the biggest fish."

"How long is your fishing expedition?" Nicole asked.

"A week, but no more than ten days because some of the guys have to be back on base before they're AWOL."

"What do you do during the off year?"

Fletcher turned on the gas grill. "Those of us who are civilians will meet once or twice a year. This past May, I invited two of my buddies to come to The Falls for the Memorial Day weekend. They marched in the parade with me, and really enjoyed the picnic afterward."

"One thing I can say about Wickham Falls is that the town officials really know how to host a celebration."

Fletcher nodded. "Word." While on active duty, he'd missed the three-day Fourth of July celebration, the Memorial Day parade and picnic, and Halloween night festivities. "Other than your navy SEAL, are you connected to any of your other buddies?"

Nicole lowered her hand. "No. I seemed to have lost touch with everyone in my NROTC class except Keith."

There was something in Nicole's tone that signaled to Fletcher she hadn't wanted to keep in touch with her former military comrades. He wondered if the death of the master sergeant had emotionally impacted her more than she wanted to acknowledge. On the other hand, when he'd seen her interacting with those who had crowded into the Den for Military Monday, she'd appeared to be in her element.

"How do you like your steak?" he asked, smoothly segueing away from the topic of the military.

"Medium well." Nicole rested her hand at the middle of Fletcher's back. "Are you sure there isn't anything I can do to help you?"

Bending slightly, Fletcher opened the fridge and took out bottles of merlot and prosecco. "Which one do you want?"

"I prefer the prosecco."

"There's a corkscrew on the table." He drew a normal breath for the first time since Nicole had touched his back. Although the gesture was an innocent one, it still had turned him on. He'd had to shift his body slightly away from her so she wouldn't detect his hard-on.

Now that he was back in control of his traitorous body, he placed a large cast-iron skillet on the stove and coated it with a couple of tablespoons of canola oil. While he waited for the oil to heat, Fletcher took a cutting board from a shelf under the stove. Once the oil was hot enough, he added the steaks and cooked them over high heat until the bottoms were crusty.

He then turned over the steaks and added butter, sprigs of thyme, rosemary and slivers of garlic to the skillet, basting the steaks with the melted butter and herbs until the steaks were medium well. Transferring the steaks to the cutting board, he let them rest for ten minutes and then placed the skewers on the grill.

It was only after installing the outdoor kitchen that Fletcher had taken a concerted interest in cooking. He had begun watching cooking channels and downloading and printing recipes off the internet. He'd had some failures, but most times what he prepared was palatable. It would take him years, if not decades, to compete with Nicole, and he was looking forward to assisting her if or when they prepared meals together.

Nicole stared up at the night sky sprinkled with stars that reminded her of diamond dust on a blanket of dark blue velvet. The smell of burning wood from the firepit, the tinkling of wind chimes and the sultry, distinctive voice of Sade singing “Sweetest Taboo” flowing from speakers set up around the patio, lulled her into a state of complete relaxation.

The dinner of garlic-buttered, herb-infused grilled steak, roasted vegetable kabobs and prosecco was nothing short of perfection. His fajitas and now the rib eye steaks were comparable to what she’d had in restaurants. Nicole hadn’t eaten too much, but she had drunk too much. She’d exceeded her two-drink limit and the result was that she did not want to get up to go inside.

“Do you plan to sleep out here all night?”

She turned to look at Fletcher reclining on the chaise next to hers. After putting away everything, he’d volunteered to walk Othello.

“May I?”

“You can, but don’t complain if you wake with bug bites. Once the citronella torches burn out, you’ll become a feast for the mosquitos.”

Nicole sat up. Many of the candles had burned out and others were sputtering. “I hope I find my way inside the house without falling on my face. I drank too much.”

Fletcher got off his recliner, leaned down and scooped Nicole up. “You don’t have to walk, babe. I’ll carry you upstairs to your bedroom.”

Wrapping her arms around his neck, she pressed her face against his muscled shoulder.

Any modicum of uncertainty vanished whenever Nicole found herself in Fletcher’s arms. She protested vehemently when he talked about protecting her, but if she was truly honest with herself, she would acknowledge it without protest.

She loved him, and was in love with him, and if circumstances had been different she would have accepted his proposal to become his wife and the mother of their children. A wry smile twisted her mouth when she recalled the number of men she'd met since enrolling in college. One she'd believed she loved enough to marry and another after she'd received her commission. As a woman she was a minority in the military and even part of a smaller number who had gone into combat, yet she'd had to return to her hometown to reunite with a man who unknowingly had captured a little piece of her heart. A man she was willing to give not only her heart but also her body.

"I don't want to sleep in my bedroom." Fletcher stopped, Nicole feeling the stiffness in his body. "I want to sleep with you."

"Do you know what you're asking?"

She smiled against his shoulder. "I know exactly what I'm saying, Fletcher. I want to sleep in your bed tonight."

"Just to sleep, Nikki?"

"Yes, if you don't have protection, because I didn't bring any condoms with me."

Fletcher realized he had to get used to the very adult Nicole Campos, who said what she wanted and said exactly what came to her mind. He was so used to women who preferred playing head games that had left him confused, exasperated and unaware their coquettish antics were a turnoff.

"I have condoms."

Nicole pressed a kiss to the column of his neck. "Can you give me time to shower and brush my teeth?"

Fletcher smiled. “Take all the time you need, sweetheart. I still have to put out the candles and the firepit.”

He carried her up the staircase and to the bedroom where she’d slept the first time she’d come to his home. He still did not want to believe how comfortable it had felt spending hours with Nicole. It was as if they’d turned back the clock to when they’d worked together on yearbook and senior class committees. It had been their responsibility to gather all the information for the yearbook and to make certain to list the various clubs, awards and future careers for all the graduating seniors.

Fletcher walked into the bedroom where he’d placed Nicole’s overnight bag and set her on her feet. Cradling her face in his hands, he lowered his head and brushed a light kiss over her parted lips. “Don’t run away,” he teased.

Rising on tiptoe, Nicole curved her arms around his neck and pulled his head down. “Never,” she whispered before taking his mouth in a passionate kiss that made the hairs on the back of his neck stand up.

Fletcher knew if she did not stop kissing him, he would take her where they stood. And making love to her without a condom was something neither of them wanted or was ready for given the consequences of an unplanned pregnancy. If or when Nicole carried their child, he wanted her to be Mrs. J. Fletcher Austen.

He forcibly removed her arms, holding her wrists firmly against her body. He met her eyes in the light coming from the lamps on the bedside tables. They were dark, her gaze steady and trusting. “Not yet, darling.”

Nicole angled her head and smiled. “Hurry back.”

Fletcher nodded. “I will.” He released her wrists, turned on his heel and walked stiffly out of the bedroom. The pulsing of his erection was painful and pleasurable at the same time. It was the second time Nicole had aroused him so much that he feared losing complete control, something he hadn't done since the onset of puberty.

He took the rear staircase and opened the door leading out to the patio. It took him less than fifteen minutes to extinguish all the candles and the torches and to douse the embers in the firepit. Flipping several wall switches, he turned off the lights in the trees and around the perimeter of the house, and the stereo system. Othello had come out of the house, and Fletcher patted his head. The canine had become his constant companion.

"It's time to go inside for the night. Tomorrow we'll play catch together." The instant the words were out, he realized he was doing what he'd teased Nicole about: he was talking to a dog. Othello trotted inside and settled down on his bed, which Fletcher had positioned between the alcove with the office and pantry.

He tapped a button, arming the security system, then turned off all the lights on the first story and climbed the staircase to the upper level. Light from under outlets throughout the house provided enough illumination for one to walk around without bumping into objects. He'd installed the LED dusk-to-dawn night-light sensors after he'd nearly broken a toe bumping into the leg of the hallway table.

Fletcher detected the scent of Nicole's bodywash as soon as he walked into his bedroom, smiling when he saw the outline of her body under the blanket. She was facing the far wall and he didn't know whether she was awake or asleep. He managed to make it to the bathroom without disturbing her, and he showered and brushed his teeth. She'd left a colorful quilted cosmetic bag on one of the shelves in the bathroom.

Soft snoring greeted him when he returned to the bedroom and slipped into bed next to Nicole. She had come to bed completely nude and the silken feel of her skin sent shock waves through his body. Resting his arm over her waist, he pulled her closer to him, her hips pressed to his groin. She stirred slightly but did not wake up.

Chapter Twelve

Nicole felt the heat and then the crush of an immovable object against her back. She opened her eyes and saw slivers of light coming through shuttered windows. She didn't want to believe she'd spent the night in Fletcher's bed and had fallen asleep without their making love.

"Good morning, Sleeping Beauty."

She felt Fletcher's moist breath on the nape of her neck. "Don't you mean Rip van Winkle?"

"Nah, beautiful. If you were Rip van Winkle, then we'd have to wait another twenty years to sleep together, and by then I just might be too old to chase you around the bedroom."

Nicole shifted slightly and attempted to turn over to face him, but couldn't move Fletcher's arm resting on her waist. She wanted to remind Fletcher that he was projecting, or maybe it was wishful thinking on his part.

He was talking about twenty years from now, while she wasn't certain the path her life would take within the next twenty months. Her former employer had extended an olive branch and was open to rehiring her. While she loathed returning, she still had to consider Preston's offer to make her a junior partner.

"You may have more trouble at fifty-five, but I'm sure you'll do okay when it comes to a footrace." She attempted to move again. "You're going to have to let me go, Fletcher, because I need to use the bathroom." The last word was barely off her tongue when he swept her off the bed, threw her over his shoulder and headed for the adjoining bath. He set her on her feet and disappeared behind a partition for the urinal, but not before she'd caught a glimpse of his lean, muscled body in all its magnificent nakedness.

Nicole did not want to believe she was sharing a bathroom with Fletcher while attempting to complete her morning ablutions. Wrapping a bath sheet around her body, she managed to relieve herself in record time. She was standing at the twin vanity, squeezing toothpaste onto her brush when Fletcher joined her. Unlike her, he hadn't covered himself.

"I didn't expect you to go caveman on me," she said, meeting his eyes in the reflection of the mirror.

Fletcher winked as he put paste on his own brush. "I didn't want you to have an accident."

"I never have accidents." He nodded, smiling as they both brushed their teeth. Nicole deliberately stared at her reflection rather than at Fletcher's. Did he not know of his effect on her standing less than three feet away, completely naked and semi-aroused? And why did she feel as if sharing the bathroom was a normal occurrence for them?

"Am I embarrassing you?"

"Why should I be embarrassed?" she asked, answering his question with one of her own.

"You keep averting your eyes."

Reaching for a paper cup from the wall dispenser, Nicole filled it with water and rinsed her mouth. "I don't want you think I'm a Peeping Thomasina."

"You don't have to concern yourself about that, Nikki. I have nothing to hide from you."

She washed her face then blotted it on a paper towel before discarding it in a gray wicker wastebasket. "So, I see," Nicole mumbled under her breath as she applied a light cover of moisturizer to her face and neck.

Fletcher gave her a sidelong glance. "I'm going to let Othello out and then make some coffee. We can drink it in bed if you want."

Nicole smiled. "That sounds like a plan." She adjusted the bath sheet over her breasts and left the bathroom. *We're like an old married couple.* The thought just popped into her head. It had taken her a while to allow a man to come into the bathroom while she'd been there. It was not because of vanity, but for the need for complete discretion to do whatever she needed to do.

However, it was different with Fletcher. Her comfort level with him was astounding, which in and of itself made him very, very special. Perhaps it also had something to do with her trusting him not to do anything she didn't want him to do. It was obvious that he wanted to make love to her, and she to him, but she felt no urgency for them to engage in the act.

Nicole pulled the nightgown she'd left on the bedroom chair the night before over her head. The white cotton garment with pale blue flowers and spaghetti straps ended at her knees. Walking over to the window, she opened the shutters and rays of brilliant sunlight flooded the room.

The landscape unfolding before her eyes was breathtaking. The tops of the mountains were shrouded in a blue haze and she could see the water spilling over the twin waterfalls that gave the town its name. Nicole had always thought of her home state as untamed and majestic. The mountainous terrain, the deep gorges and waterfalls, the natural forests that had become a hunter's nirvana for hunting deer, and the many rivers and streams where fishermen caught small- and largemouth bass, channel catfish and walleye. Then there were the numerous streams, brooks and lakes where children learned to swim rather than in an indoor pool.

She'd told Fletcher that she had become so accustomed to the pulsing energy of her adopted city that she could not envision ever living in a place like Wickham Falls again. When, she mused, had she become so closeminded that it was all or nothing?

Nicole had returned to The Falls for the first time to check on Reggie in March, and then returned again in May to coincide with the end of the school year. It was almost October and it was only now that she realized she'd come home. She still slept in the bedroom where she'd grown up, and the memories of coming home to find her grandmother baking cookies were revived when she baked cookies for her nephews.

She loved Fletcher and had fallen in love with him, but knew that wasn't enough for her to commit to a future with him. At least not yet. There were other factors to consider. Nicole had moved to Florida to be closer to her aging parents. They were still in good health and independent, but she knew there could come a time when she would have to assume the responsibility of perhaps becoming a caregiver for her mother, father or both. It was different with Fletcher because he lived close to his parents. He'd even bought a house in Wickham Falls because he was slated to take over the family business.

Moving away from the window, she pulled back the covers on the bed, smoothed out the sheet and blankets. After plumping up the pillows, she placed them against the quilted headboard and turned down the duvet.

"You didn't have to do that."

She turned around at the sound of Fletcher's voice and saw him standing in the doorway holding a cup of steaming coffee in each hand. He'd pulled on a pair of shorts, but had left his chest bare. She thought him incredibly handsome and masculine with the stubble on his lean jaw. "I don't like getting back into an unmade bed."

He smiled and a fine network of lines fanned out around his laughing eyes. "I'll remember that in the future."

Nicole got into bed and took the mug he handed to her. "That smells wonderful."

Fletcher slipped in beside her. "There's nothing better than the smell of brewing coffee and broiling bacon in the morning."

She touched her mug to his and took a sip. "You're so right about that."

"What do you want for breakfast?" he asked.

"Nothing right now. The coffee is good."

Fletcher rested his head against the stack of pillows under his back and shoulders. "When I let Othello out, he took off like a shot after a rabbit."

Nicole let out a gasp. "I hope he didn't catch it."

"I don't think so because he came back right away without anything in his mouth."

"Where is he now?"

"I left him on the patio with a bowl of water. He seems very content to lie in the sun."

"Keith's going to be shocked to find that his canine warrior is just a big pussy cat."

Fletcher crossed his feet at the ankles, bringing her eyes to linger on the scars on his right leg. "Do the scars turn you off?" he asked.

Nicole shook her head. It was obvious he'd caught her staring. "Of course not. Why would you think that?"

"Because it's the first time you've seen them."

She moved closer and kissed his shoulder. "And it definitely won't be the last, because I intend to sleep with my man every chance I get."

"Am I really your man, Nicole?"

"Of course, you are. If you weren't, I wouldn't be in bed with you." Fletcher had no idea how many overtures she'd had from men who'd felt she was obligated to sleep with them because she'd agreed to share dinner or a drink, while believing she would become their dessert.

Fletcher took the mug from her hand and set it beside his on the table and then he cradled her face in his hands and kissed her. Nicole did not remember when he'd deepened the kiss or when her arms went around his strong neck. She could not recall when he'd divested her of the nightgown or when he'd shed his shorts. What she did remember was the feathery kisses on her face before they moved lower to the pulse in her throat and then even lower to her breasts and belly. She was helpless to stop the groans of frustration when she wanted Fletcher to stop kissing her and assuage the pulsing between her thighs.

Fletcher reached into the drawer on the night table and removed a condom. He'd wanted to go slow and engage in a lengthy foreplay before penetrating Nicole but knew that wasn't going to happen after he'd waited half his life to claim the girl who had ensnared him in a web of longing that had waned and was then revived once he'd come face-to-face with her again. He didn't know what it was about Nicole that had him lusting after her like a man deprived of food for long periods of time.

He slipped the condom over his erection and, moving over Nicole, he parted her thighs with his knee and slowly, gently, eased his hardness into her tight, moist flesh. She let out a gasp, then a moan once he fully sheathed himself inside her. His world stood still, then spun on its axis when her legs went around his waist, allowing him deeper penetration. All Fletcher could think of was that the wait was more than worth it. All the women he'd known were now nameless and faceless, and his past, because the woman writhing under him was everything he wanted and needed.

Fletcher struggled not to ejaculate. The runaway pumping of Nicole's heart against his chest, the contractions squeezing his erect penis and the soft moans near his ears when he buried his face in the pillow cradling her head, told him she was close to climaxing.

"Let it go, baby," he groaned. "Please."

He didn't have to wait long when he felt her orgasms

overlap one another at the same time he released his dammed-up passion. Fletcher loved Nicole more than he could have imagined loving someone.

"I love you," he whispered over and over until it became a litany.

Cradling his face between her palms, Nicole kissed his mouth and the end of his nose. "I love you, too."

A lump settled in Fletcher's throat as he struggled to swallow. They loved each other, but to what end? He'd proposed marriage, promised to protect Nicole, but he suspected there was something else in her life that wouldn't permit her to share it with him. He'd waited a long time for this moment—to make love with her—but wondered how much longer he would have to wait for her to decide whether she would move back to Wickham Falls permanently.

In that instant Fletcher made himself a promise. He would wait for her brother to complete his treatment and come back to The Falls. If Nicole decided to return to Florida, then Fletcher knew it was over between them.

He reversed positions, her legs sandwiched between his outstretched ones. "Are you ready to eat now?"

Nicole rested her chin on his chest and smiled up at him. "Soon." Reaching up, she traced the outline of a colorful tattoo on the underside of his left arm. "When did you get this one?"

Fletcher peered at what she'd pointed to. "That was to celebrate becoming Special Forces." One by one, he identified each of the tattoos and when he'd gotten them.

"Do you plan to get another one?"

He shook his head. "No. I have enough. You're next."

Nicole held up her right arm stamped with USMC in small black letters. "I'm done. Everyone told me once you get one, you'll want another, but I proved them wrong."

Fletcher found himself opening up to Nicole about his experiences during a couple of his deployments. He found it odd that she was content to listen and not contribute to the conversation. After a while he realized she'd fallen asleep. Easing her down to the mattress, he pulled the sheet up over her body and minutes later joined her in a sated sleep for lovers.

Nicole felt her heart stop and start up again when she saw the name and number appear on her cell phone screen. She answered the call after the second ring. The only time Keith's sister called her was when he experienced a meltdown.

"Hello, Rachel."

"Hi, Nicole. Keith's good, but it's my kids I'm calling about. They both have strep throat, along with a bunch of other kids in their school, so I'm calling everyone and telling them to stay away. Keith's disappointed that he won't get to see you, but I told him we'll get together at another time."

"How's he doing?"

"He's been seeing our next-door neighbor and they appear to be quite serious."

Nicole pumped her fist. "Good for him."

"I think it's good for both of them. She's a single mother with a four-year-old daughter who adores my brother. I wouldn't be surprised if he asked her to marry him."

Nicole smiled although Rachel couldn't see her. "That's really serious."

"Tell me about it."

Nicole had been looking forward to seeing Keith again, but the mere mention of strep throat was enough to keep her away. She chatted with Rachel for a few more minutes and then ended the call. Leaning back in her chair, she stared at the framed prints on the opposite wall in the office. This was her weekend to have Luke and Daniel and they'd been excited when she'd told them they were going on a road trip.

Picking up the phone, she tapped Fletcher's number. It rang five times before going to voice mail. "This weekend's plans are canceled. Call me back and I'll fill you in."

She and Fletcher jealously shielded their time together by staying at home whenever Daniel and Luke spent the weekend with their grandparents. They were content to sleep in late, cook and eat together, listen and dance to music and make endless love. It was uncanny that she found them to be so compatible and she knew, however long they would be involved, their relationship was one she would never forget.

Fletcher drove up to the house in Beckley and got out of his car, smiling at the man who'd called him to come and look at an old car stored in a shed on his property. He extended his hand. "Fletcher Austen."

The short stocky man with a long graying ponytail, wearing a black-and-red-plaid shirt and bibbed jeans, took his hand. "Dave Nichols. Thank you for coming down. When I told my cousin that my wife has been threatening to leave me if I don't get rid of a car and tear down the shed, he mentioned your name. Right now, my marriage means a lot more to me than a car, even if it is considered a classic."

"I never turn down an offer to look at a classic vehicle." He followed Dave around to the back of the house and down a path to the shed. When he unlocked the doors and removed the tarp, Fletcher couldn't stop grinning.

Dave crossed his arms over his chest. "Are you familiar with this beauty?"

Fletcher nodded. When most boys were into graphic comics, he was reading *Car and Driver*, *Motor Trend* and *Road & Track*, magazines his father had subscribed to. "It's a 1963 Buick Riviera with top speeds of 125 miles per hour. Its V-8 engine can go from zero to sixty in 8.0 seconds. The only drawback is economy. You can only get twelve miles per gallon."

Dave smiled. "You really know your cars."

"I try," Fletcher said modestly. "Does it run?"

"Wouldn't know. It belonged to one of my uncles who gave it to me before he moved to California in 1983. I haven't moved it in more than thirty years."

Fletcher rubbed his stubble as he peered into the passenger-side window. The black vinyl interior was as pristine as the burgundy exterior. "How many miles on it?"

"The last time I started it up before putting it in the shed, I think it was about 44,000."

"You have all the documents listing you as the owner?" Dave nodded. "How much do you want for it?"

"I'll take a couple of thousand just to get it off the property."

Fletcher stood straight. "You know it's worth a lot more than that." He did not want to cheat the man, because he wanted to continue the family's reputation as respectable and trustworthy businessmen.

"Right now, it's worth nothing to me because I don't drive it and I need to take down the shed to make space to put in an addition on the house. I have the papers in the house."

Fletcher knew he could easily sell the vehicle for more than twenty-five thousand, but there was something about the Riviera's design that made him want it for himself. The car had a European look with a grille that was very similar to the Ferrari 250GT.

"I'll give you twice that amount. Once the driver comes with a flatbed to pick up the car, he'll give you a bank check for five thousand. Fair enough?"

Dave's head nodded like a bobblehead doll as flush suffused his fair complexion. "It's more than fair. Thank you, brother."

"You're most welcome, brother." Fletcher retreated to the Acadia after Dave had signed the necessary documents transferring ownership of the Riviera to him, and picked up the cell phone he'd left on the passenger seat. He'd missed a call from Nicole. He listened to her message and promptly called her back. "What's up, beautiful?" He listened while she revealed her conversation with her friend's sister. He heard the disappointment in her voice, but knew strep throat was not only highly contagious but painful.

"I know the boys are going to be bummed, so I'll have to come up with something to keep them busy because I don't like keeping them in the house over the weekend. They get enough of that when they go to their grandparents'."

"Would you mind if I take them, along with Othello, hiking over to the falls?"

"Are you certain that's what you want to do, Fletcher?"

"Yes. You're welcome to come with us."

"No, thank you. It sounds more like a boys' adventure. My contribution will be to fill their backpacks with something to sustain them until you guys get back."

"What about my backpack?" Fletcher asked, smiling.

"If you have one, then I'll make enough for you."

"Thank you, my love."

"You're welcome, Fletcher."

He knew Nicole was still at work and wondered if she had someone in her office and wasn't able to respond in kind. "I miss you, baby," he whispered into the cell. "Talk to you later."

"Same here."

She'd hung up. It was a full thirty seconds before he did the same. Fletcher had exhausted his repertoire of endearments until he'd stopped searching for a new one. His father talked about being the happiest man in the world because he'd fallen in love and married Fletcher's mother, while Fletcher wondered why loving Nicole had led to angst and pain.

He felt in his heart that she did love him; and in the lingering throes of their lovemaking, she always whispered how much she loved him. However, she was very careful not to exhibit any sign of affection whenever they interacted with her nephews. The wall would go up and she'd relate to him as a friend and nothing more.

They continued to attend church services together and many of the worshippers no longer stared or whispered whenever they sat together. His mother continued to question him about his relationship with Nicole, wanting to know when he was going to bring her around, but Fletcher kept coming up with excuses why that wasn't possible. He knew Carla wanted more grandchildren—who didn't live hundreds of miles away—and he'd become her last hope.

He didn't want his mother to pin her hopes on him giving her more grandchildren, because he wasn't certain whether his love for Nicole was enough to make her change her mind and return to Wickham Falls.

Chapter Thirteen

After Fletcher returned from his hiking outing with her nephews, Nicole did not get to talk to or to see him as often as she had in the past. His father had taken eight weeks off to spend a month in Michigan and then in Texas so he and his wife could visit with their children and grandchildren, leaving Fletcher to open and close the business.

He continued to fulfill his commitment to mentor Luke and Daniel on the weekends they did not go to Mineral Springs. They'd spent hours with him in the garage on the property as he worked on his latest classic car acquisition. He'd installed new seats in the Studebaker and sold it to one of his regular collectors. He has also completed his assignment as a part-time, fill-in paramedic.

The weather had not cooperated for Halloween with a steady drizzle that canceled hayrides and bonfires.

Many of the activities had to be held in the basement of the church, including face painting and games for the children.

Nicole had brought pumpkins from a farm stand and enlisted her nephews to carve funny and macabre faces; using battery-powered candles, their creations decorated the windows at the front of the house. She'd boiled the seeds, let them dry out and then toasted them with olive oil before she sprinkled the golden-brown seeds with sea salt.

She had planned to prepare Thanksgiving dinner for the boys and Fletcher, but he'd declined, telling her he was closing the business for the holiday weekend and flying down to Texas to be with his parents and his brother's family. The Clarkes had invited her to celebrate Thanksgiving with them, and she'd accepted the overture.

Nicole felt a modicum of guilt that she had not spent much time with her brother's in-laws. However, it appeared their former acrimony at her controlling Reggie's finances had vanished when they'd welcomed her as a member of their family.

She lay on the love seat in the family room, watching a Hallmark movie she had seen before but was loath to turn the channel because it was one of her favorites. It was late December and the channel had advertised a number of new titles.

Othello suddenly stood and began whining.

Immediately, Nicole was alert. Her nephews were away for the weekend and Fletcher had called to say he wouldn't be able to see her because he had to finish rebuilding the engine on a car he'd promised to deliver to a client the following week.

"What is it, boy?" Othello continued to pace back and forth until she got up. "Okay, I'm coming." She followed him to the front door. When she peered through the security eye, she saw Fletcher staring back at her. She opened the door and, before she could say anything, he swept her up off her feet. He closed the door with his shoulder at the same time he took her mouth in an explosive kiss that threatened to draw the very breath out of her lungs.

There was an urgency to his kiss that both excited and frightened her at the same time. They had never made love in her house. He took the stairs two at a time. When he finally released her mouth, Nicole struggled to catch her breath.

"What are you doing?" she breathed.

"I plan to make love to the woman I love," he whispered in her ear.

"Fletcher..."

"Don't worry, baby. I have protection."

"You don't need protection. I'm on the Pill."

No further words were spoken as Fletcher placed her on the bed and undressed them both in record time. There was no prolonged foreplay, as in their previous encounters, as she opened her legs and welcomed him into her body. The pleasure he aroused in her was so explosive that Nicole was left gasping in the sweetest agony she had never experienced before.

"What are you doing to me?" Fletcher rasped in her ear after he turned on the bedside lamp.

She smiled. "I should be asking you the same thing."

He rolled off her body and lay beside her. "The only thing I'm doing is loving you."

Nicole laced their fingers together. "I'm going to miss you when I take the boys to Florida for Christmas."

"We still have another few days before you leave, so let's try to make some more incredible memories until you get back."

"Like now?" she said teasingly.

"Yes, baby."

She sobered. "What are you going to do for Christmas?"

"I thought about driving to Texas again, but I decided to hang around here."

Nicole sat up. "You're going to spend Christmas alone?"

Fletcher patted his chest over his heart. "I'm not alone. I have you here."

She rested her hand over his, marveling at how much smaller it looked when compared to his. "I think you've become a certified romantic."

Pushing up into a seated position, Fletcher rested his back on the padded headboard. "I have you to thank for that. I know you're going to be leaving in a few days, so I decided to bring your gift over tonight." He reached for the jeans on the floor and removed a small foil-wrapped box. "Merry Christmas, darling."

Placing a hand over her mouth and, biting down on her lip, Nicole struggled not to become emotional. The box was too large for a ring, but she knew it had to contain a piece of jewelry. Her steady fingers belied her inner anxiety when she removed the paper and opened the velvet box. Inside, on a bed of white satin, lay a delicate diamond heart pendant. *I'm giving you my heart to keep* was calligraphed on a narrow strip of pink parchment.

Nicole straddled Fletcher's lap and pressed her bare breasts to his chest. "Thank you, my love. I will treasure it always." She kissed him, smiling and wanting to tell him she would love him for an eternity. "I have something to give you, too."

Fletcher cradled her face. "You didn't have to get me anything."

She scrambled off the bed and walked over to a closet, returning with a box wrapped in festive paper. "It's not much. It's hard to shop for a man who appears to have everything he wants."

Fletcher stared at Nicole. He wanted to tell her that she was wrong. He wanted her—not just her body but all of her. "Let me be the judge of that."

He removed the paper and opened a box with vinyl records in protective sleeves. His jaw dropped. She had given him several rare recordings of 1940s jazz greats.

"Where did you find these?"

"I'm not telling."

"Did you go to a collector?"

"I'm still not telling. Just be gracious and accept them."

He shook his head. "You just don't know how long I've been searching for these."

"Search no more, darling. Just enjoy them."

Fletcher kissed her mussed hair. "I'm going to wait until you come back and we'll listen to them together." He paused. "I'd like to ask a favor of you."

"What is it?"

"Let Othello stay with me until you get back."

Nicole went completely still. "Really?"

"Yes, really. Pop always closes the shop for vacation

between Christmas and New Year, so I thought Othello and I could hang out and bond some more."

"If you bond any more, he'll be sleeping in the bed with you."

"That's a thought," Fletcher said as he winked at Nicole.

A beat passed. "I'll let him stay on one condition."

"And what's that?"

Nicole gave him a long, penetrating stare. "That you promise you won't let him sleep on the bed with you."

Smiling, Fletcher gave her a snappy salute. "I promise, Captain."

Her smile matched his. "At ease, Sergeant."

He took Nicole in his arms again and held her until he felt relaxed completely. Fletcher did not know why he had the nagging fear that Nicole would leave and not come back. But understanding her bond with Othello, he also knew she would not abandon him. It did not dawn on him until later that her nephews were enrolled in Johnson County schools, which meant she would be forced to return to allow them to complete the rest of the school year.

Man up! the silent voice in his head shouted at him. He'd overcome the physical and mental rigors to become a Special Forces soldier, had survived multiple deployments, and now he was quivering like an abused animal because he feared losing the only woman he had ever loved.

Fletcher knew he had to believe she was coming back and, that when she did, he would be forced to face his future with or without Nicole.

Nicole sat across the table from her brother, the joy she felt reflected her eyes. Reggie had regained the weight he had lost. He had also completed four months of his stint and, fortunately, had not relapsed.

Luke and Daniel hung on to his neck as if they feared that if they let him go he would disappear.

Reggie, given a day pass to celebrate Christmas with his family and knowing he had to return to the facility by eight that night, patted his sons on their heads. "Boys, you're going to have to let me go because I need to talk to your auntie."

Elizabeth Campos stood. "Come in the kitchen with Grammie, so your daddy and auntie can have some privacy."

Luke stared up at his grandmother. "Are they going to talk about me?"

Elizabeth dropped a kiss on his hair. "I don't think so, baby."

Nicole waited until they were alone to study her brother. She had always thought him incredibly handsome—as had most of the girls in The Falls and Springs—with his even features and large dark eyes framed by lashes better suited for a woman. She'd always teased him, saying he'd gotten her lashes. His hair was grayer now and there were a few more lines around his eyes. He also moved slower as a result of the accident.

Reggie patted the chair beside him. "Come and sit here, because what I want to tell you should go no further than this table."

Nicole got up and took the chair Daniel had vacated, praying Reggie wasn't going to tell her something she didn't want or need to hear. "What is it?"

Reggie lowered his voice and his head. "I want you to put the house on the market. I've decided not to return to

The Falls. I've asked Dad if he would become a backup sponsor when my regular sponsor isn't available. Even though he hasn't gone through recovery he's agreed to step in."

Nicole's eyes were as round as silver dollars. "Does Mom know about this?"

"Yes. It was her suggestion when I talked about not going back to West Virginia."

"Where will you live once you're discharged?"

"There are a few condos for sale not too far from here."

"You can stay with me until you find a place," Nicole volunteered. "I have two extra bedrooms, so there's enough room for you and the boys to stay until you find something permanent." She paused. "What about Daniel and Luke? Don't you want them to finish their school year in The Falls?"

"No. I've researched a private school close to here, with small classes that will provide individual instruction if they need it. They will also have access to a lot of extracurricular activities included in the tuition." He dropped an arm over her shoulders. "You've given up your life to take care of my sons, for that I'll never be able to repay you, Nikki."

Nicole rested her head on her brother's shoulder. "You don't have to repay me. We're family and that's all that matters."

"But you gave up your career to take care of my boys."

"I gave up a position, not a career, Reggie. Remember, I'm licensed to practice law in several states, so I don't think I'm going to have a problem getting another position."

"I haven't thought about that. How long do you think it will take to sell the house?"

"I don't know," Nicole said. "I'll call the Realtor tomorrow and find out if anyone is looking to buy in The Falls. The upside is the house has been updated *and* is in what is considered an upscale section of the town. How much are you asking, Reggie?"

He shook his head. "It doesn't matter. I'll go along with whatever the prevailing rate is."

Nicole was aware of how much her brother was worth and knew he wouldn't haggle with a buyer about the profit he could derive from the sale of the house that had been a wedding gift from his parents. "I'll also contact a moving company to pack up everything and ship it down here for storage until you find something you want."

Reggie pulled Nicole closer and kissed her cheek. "Thank you, baby sis."

She blinked back tears. It had been a long time since he'd called her. "We're family, so there's no need to thank me."

It was later, after her father had driven Reggie back to the facility, that Nicole sat with her mother on the balcony overlooking the Intracoastal. A warm breeze flittered across her face and the smell of salt water reminded her of what she had missed since she'd gone back to Wickham Falls. It felt good to go barefoot and wear shorts instead of boots and wool slacks.

"Why do you look so down in the mouth when you're in love?"

She turned to look at Elizabeth. Her liberally streaked gray hair framed a slender light brown face with an elegant ridge of cheekbones. "Why do you think I'm in love?"

"Because my grandsons can't stop talking about you and Fletcher Austen."

Nicole half sat on the recliner. "What did they say?" She and Fletcher had been so careful not to flaunt their love for each other around her nephews.

"They said that Uncle Fletcher is in love with their auntie Nikki."

Her eyebrows shot up. "They told you he said that?"

"Not in so many words. Kids are a lot more perceptive than we give them credit for, Nicole. They see things we don't think they see and draw their own conclusions. Are you in love with him?"

Nicole had never lied to her mother and she wasn't going to begin now. "Yes."

"And?"

"And what, Mom?"

"What are you going to do about it?"

"Nothing. After I sell the house, I'm coming back to restart my career. Dad mentioned he'd spoken to a lawyer who was looking for an assistant for his family practice. He said I would be perfect for the position."

Elizabeth's hands curled into tight fists. "When did my kids lose all semblance of common sense? I stayed on my knees when you and Reginald were teenagers, praying that you wouldn't go the wrong way. Reginald waits until his old ass is thirty-eight to get hooked on drugs. Meanwhile you find a man who loves you and all you can talk about is working in some firm."

"Mom! That's not fair what you just said about Reggie."

The older woman's dark eyes grew wide. "Don't you

dare talk to me about my son. I'd warned him over and over that he was taking too many pain meds, and that his priority was taking care of his kids now that they didn't have a mama. He kept telling me, 'I got this.' And what did it get him? Overdosing where his kids could see him unresponsive on the bathroom floor. When you become a parent, Nicole, you cannot think of only yourself."

"I'm not a parent, Mom."

"You think not? Do you realize that's what you've been doing these past months? You took care of Danny and Luke, worked for Preston McAvoy, cooked and cleaned the house, like millions of women do every day. And now that you've met a man who I assume loves you, as evidenced by that necklace you try to hide, you start talking out of the side of your mouth about a career. You can have a career anywhere, but when true love comes along, you better hold on to it, Nicole. If not, you'll be left wanting, waiting and wishing for the rest of your life."

"I'll think about it, Mom."

"Don't think too long, Nicole. We're leaving tomorrow to board the ship. Are you going to stay here until we get back?"

Nicole nodded. "I plan to."

She didn't want to leave Miami without seeing her nephews. Her mother had contacted the school where Reggie wanted to enroll them and had gotten all the necessary papers for him to authorize the Johnson County schools to download the documents needed for registration. And because Nicole currently had temporary power of attorney for his finances until he completed treatment, the elder Camposes had written a check to cover their grandchildren's tuition.

* * *

Nicole answered her cell phone. Fletcher had decided to FaceTime her, showing him and Othello romping in the newly fallen snow. "How much snow did you get?"

"Only three inches. How's the weather in sunny Florida?"

"Warm. It went to eighty-five yesterday."

He smiled. "Show-off. You look as if you've been in the sun. Your face is darker."

"I went to the beach to read… I need to tell you something."

He sat in the snow with Othello. "I hope it's good news."

Nicole told him about her brother permanently relocating to Florida and enrolling his sons in a private school.

A frown furrowed Fletcher's forehead. "How did they take the news?"

"You know kids. They're a lot more adaptable than adults. Once they saw the beach and ocean, they did the happy dance."

"What about you, Nikki? When are you coming back?"

"I'll be back right after the New Year. I've already notified Mrs. Riley to list the house, so I don't know how long it will take before the sale is final. By the way, I may have a job here in Miami. I had an interview yesterday. So far, I have a good feeling about it."

"Do you plan to accept it if they offer it to you?"

"Probably. They didn't mention salary, so that may be a factor. I also told them I wouldn't be able start for a while, which didn't sit too well with the interviewer. If they really want me, then they'll just have to wait."

He smiled. “It looks as if I’ll get the chance to hang out with my buddy a little longer.”

“Is he sleeping on the bed with you, Fletcher?”

“I’m sorry, Nicole, but I have another call.”

“No, you don’t!” she shouted at the screen. “You promised me you…” Her words trailed off when Fletcher hung up on her. Nicole curbed the urge to stomp her foot like she’d done as a child.

Fletcher was waiting on the porch when she drove up. She’d called to give him an approximate time of her arrival. Not only was she exhausted, she was also hungry from the long drive. She’d stopped once to refuel, stretch her legs and have a cup of soup with a sandwich. Pangs of hunger had attacked her when she least expected.

Othello came to greet her and she scratched him behind his ears. “You missed your mama, didn’t you, boy?”

Fletcher pulled her into his arms. “Not as much as his papa did.” He brushed a kiss over her parted lips. “You look exhausted.”

“The only thing I want is a bed and a hot bath, and not necessarily in that order.”

“Don’t you want anything to eat?”

“No, thank you. Right now, I’m not as hungry as I am tired.”

He led her inside the house and up the staircase to his bedroom. “I’ll run the water while you get out of those clothes.”

When Nicole told him that she’d wanted a bath, she hadn’t expected him to join her in the Jacuzzi. He’d turned off the light and the only illumination came from a full moon shining through the skylight. She lay, eyes closed, with the back of her head on his chest. "I missed you so much," she whispered.

"That goes twice for me, babe."

She shifted to face him, smiling. "Please make love to me, Fletcher."

Nicole knew she was begging him to love her because she was so confused about her feelings for him. She loved him, but her life was more complicated now than it had been before Christmas. Reggie's decision to sell the family home and permanently live in Florida meant the Camposes severing all ties with Wickham Falls. And the company that wanted to hire her had offered more money than she'd had in mind, which only served to exacerbate her dilemma.

The heated swirling waters in the garden tub added to their buoyancy when Fletcher eased his erection inside her. She moaned and threw her head back in ecstasy. Why, she thought, did he have the power to make every man she'd met and known cease to exist? She knew the answer as soon as the thought formed in her head—because he was the only man she'd ever loved.

Fletcher's lovemaking was slow and deliberate, as if he wanted it to last forever, but passion was not to be denied when they climaxed at the same time. They lay motionless until their heart rates slowed to a normal rhythm. She allowed him to wash her body and then lift her out of the tub to blot the moisture from her body.

Nicole did remember him tucking her into bed, but nothing beyond that. She woke up the next morning to discover that Fletcher wasn't in the bed with her.

Tossing back the blankets, she swung her legs over the side of the mattress and walked to the bathroom.

She stared at her reflection in the mirror. The Southern sun had darkened her face and chest to a rich nut brown.

Nicole completed her morning ablutions, and when she returned to the bedroom, she found Fletcher in bed, balancing a tray across his lap. He pointed to one on the nightstand on her side of the bed.

"Yours is over there."

She got into bed and brushed a kiss over his mouth before settling her tray on her lap. "You're definitely a keeper."

Chapter Fourteen

Nicole had tried to convince herself to stay, but it was becoming more and more difficult to listen to her heart. The house sold within six weeks of being on the market and the entire contents were now in a Miami storage facility.

Reggie had completed his six-month treatment program and had signed up for counseling sessions three times a week. He liked living in her town home and had submitted an application for an available unit across the road. Her nephews had adjusted to their new school and liked that all the students wore the same uniform.

She stared up at Fletcher and tried to read his impassive expression. He hadn't asked her again to stay, and she knew he wouldn't. "I guess this is goodbye until the next time."

"Will there be a next time, Nicole? There is nothing in The Falls for you to come back to."

Nicole reacted as if he'd struck her across the face. "How can you say that?"

"I said it because it's true and you know it. You better head out before it gets too late."

She watched as he turned and went into his house, closing the door and shutting her out of his life forever. When the time had come closer to her departure, they had become polite strangers. They slept without making love and shared meals, but she was more than aware that the intimacy they'd shared was gone and would never return.

Fletcher was right about it getting late. It was six in the morning and she had a fourteen-hour drive ahead of her. The Pathfinder was loaded with her luggage and all that Othello would need during the trip.

Nicole got in behind the wheel, backed out of the driveway and onto the road. If she'd looked in the rearview mirror, she would've seen Fletcher standing at the window, watching her drive away.

Nicole got up to help her mother clear the table when she felt a sharp pain in her side. "Oh!" she gasped in an attempt to catch her breath.

Elizabeth turned to look at her. "Are you all right?"

She shook her head. "I don't know. I just felt a pain as if someone was ripping out my insides."

"Omigod! You're bleeding!" Elizabeth screamed.

Nicole looked to find droplets of blood trickling down her legs. "I can't be. It's not time for my period."

Elizabeth rushed over to her and eased her down to the floor. "Don't move. I'm going to call for an ambulance."

She lay on the cool marble floor, praying. Did she have a tumor that had ruptured? Or even worse… Nicole forced herself not to think of the worst possible scenario.

It seemed as if hours passed when it was actually only minutes before the EMTs arrived and wheeled her out of the condo and into an awaiting ambulance. The technician kept talking to her while he checked her vitals. She answered in monotone because she was beginning to feel weaker and weaker.

Her mother held her hand. "You're going to be okay, baby."

Her eyelids fluttered. "Mama, if I die, promise me you'll give me a military funeral. And I want to be buried in Arlington."

"Stop it, Nicole. You're not going to die. Not for a long time."

"Tell Fletcher I will marry him if he still wants me."

Tests revealed she was pregnant, despite taking a contraceptive, and there was the possibility she might lose her baby. Everything became a blur as she was wheeled through Emergency and into an operating room. The bright light hurt her eyes, and after a while, everything faded when she was sedated.

Nicole had lost track of time. When she was finally lucid, she saw Fletcher sitting on the chair next to her bed. A short beard covered his face. "What are you doing here?"

Rising slightly, he leaned over the bed to kiss her parched lips. "Your mother called me to say you were in the hospital and to tell me that you wanted to marry me, but only if I still want you."

She combed her fingers through her hair with her free hand. A needle was taped to her left hand, with a tube hooked up to a bag of clear liquid flowing into her vein. "I told her that?"

"I supposed you thought you were going to die."

A half smile parted her lips. "Well, it looks as if I'm still here." She ran her free hand over her hair. "I can't believe I got pregnant even though I was on the Pill." Now she knew why she'd experienced recurring pangs of hunger.

Fletcher smiled. "Pill or not, you're carrying our baby."

Nicole couldn't stop the tears from filling her eyes and streaming down her face. It was apparent nature had conspired against her. And Fletcher had said enough times for it to be branded on her brain that he did not want to father a child unless he was married. Well, she thought, he was about to get his wish.

"Do you still want me?" she asked through sniffles.

He blotted her tears with a tissue. "Of course, I want you, Nikki. There was never a time when I didn't want you. I want to marry you, but that's not going to happen until you're stronger. Meanwhile you're not to pick up anything heavier than a feather. I'm going to stay in a hotel until you're discharged."

"You don't have to do that, Fletcher. You can stay at my place."

"What about your brother and nephews?"

"They'll make room for you. That way y'all can have a bro-fest. By the way, how far along am I?"

"They're estimating you're at least eight weeks."

Nicole smiled as she cradled her flat belly. "Eight weeks and I never had any symptoms. I can't believe I'm going to become a mother."

"She's awake."

Nicole turned to find her mother and father walking

into the room. Elizabeth kissed Fletcher while Andrew shook his hand.

"How are you feeling?"

"Good, Mom. I'm still a little sleepy."

"They probably gave you something to relax you. I spoke to the doctor, and he says they'd like to keep you for another two days before he signs off on your discharge," Elizabeth said, leaning over to press her mouth to Nicole's ear.

"I guess I'll have to take it easy for a couple of months," Nicole said loud enough for the others in the room to hear.

"How about the next seven months?" Fletcher countered. "Once you get back to Wickham Falls, you're not going to do anything more strenuous than putting your feet up. You won't have to clean the house, shop for food, do laundry or cook."

Andrew gave Fletcher a fist bump. "You tell her, son. What you have to do from the onset is put your foot down and let your woman know you mean business."

Elizabeth stared at her husband as if he'd lost his mind. "Stop it, Andrew, and stay out of their business. You'll get Fletcher in more trouble than he can shake a stick at."

Nicole laughed. "Fletcher can have his way until after I have the baby. Then it will be my turn to pull rank. Right, Sergeant?"

Fletcher gave her a snappy salute. "Yes, Captain."

Everyone dissolved into laughter, and they were still laughing when Reggie came in with his sons. Nicole told them they were going to have another cousin before the end of the year, and that she and Fletcher were planning to marry sometime in the spring.

Luke looked at Fletcher and then at his aunt. "I

thought you were already married. That's why we called him Uncle Fletcher."

Fletcher rubbed Luke's head. "Before I was your play uncle, but when I marry your aunt Nikki, it will be for real and for keeps."

"Are you getting married here?" Daniel asked.

Nicole met Fletcher's eyes. "No. I think we should marry in Wickham Falls. I'd like a small, private gathering with just family and friends. I think Fletcher's patio would be the perfect setting for a wedding."

Fletcher winked at her. "I agree."

Nicole closed her eyes. She'd never known, when she'd rejected Fletcher as a prom date, that he would eventually become her husband and the father of her children. It was obvious that good things come to those who wait.

* * * * *

Be on the lookout for the next
Wickham Falls Weddings book, available from
Harlequin Special Edition in January 2020!

And in the meantime,
catch up with all your favorite Falls residents
in these other great books in the series:

Home to Wickham Falls
Claiming the Captain's Baby
Her Wickham Falls SEAL
The Sheriff of Wickham Falls

Available now wherever Harlequin
Special Edition books and ebooks are sold!

Alyssa Santangelo has no memory of the past seven years—including her divorce—but she remembers her love for Connor Bravo. One way or another, she's going to get her husband back.

Read on for a sneak preview of
A Husband She Couldn't Forget,
the next book in Christine Rimmer's
The Bravos of Valentine Bay miniseries.

An accident. I've been in an accident. The stitches they'd put in her knee throbbed dully, her cheeks and forehead burned and she had a mild headache. Every time she took a breath, she remembered that the seat belt had not been very nice to her.

She must have made a noise, because as she sagged back to the pillow again, Dante flinched and opened his eyes. "Hey, little sis." He'd always called her that, even though she was second eldest, after him. "How you feelin'?"

"Everything aches," she grumbled. "But I'll live." Longing flooded her for the comfort of her husband's strong arms. She needed him near. He would soothe all her pains and ease her weird, formless fears. "Where's Connor gotten off to?"

HSEEXP0919

Dante's mouth fell half-open, as though in bafflement at her question. "Connor?"

He looked so befuddled, she couldn't help chuckling a little, even though laughing made her chest and ribs hurt. "Yeah. Connor. You know, that guy I married nine years ago—my husband, your brother-in-law?"

Dante sat up. He also continued to gape at her like she was a few screwdrivers short of a full tool kit. "Uh, what's going on? You think you're funny?"

"Funny? Because I want my husband?" She bounced back up to a sitting position. "What exactly is happening here? I mean it, Dante. Be straight with me. Where's Connor?"